Sharon Kendrick

THE SHEIKH'S HEIR

TORONTO NEW YORK LONDON
AMSTERDAM PARIS SYDNEY HAMBURG
STOCKHOLM ATHENS TOKYO MILAN MADRID
PRAGUE WARSAW BUDAPEST AUCKLAND

ISBN-13: 978-0-373-13072-6

THE SHEIKH'S HEIR

Special thanks and acknowledgment are given to Sharon Kendrick for her contribution to The Santina Crown series.

This edition published by arrangement with Harlequin Books S.A.

For questions and comments about the quality of this book please contact us at Customer_eCare@Harlequin.ca.

www.Harlequin.com

Printed in U.S.A.

THE SANTINA CROWN

Royalty has never been so scandalous!

STOP THE PRESS—*Crown prince in shock marriage*

The tabloid headlines…

When Crown Prince Alessandro of Santina proposes to paparazzi favorite Allegra Jackson it promises to be *the* social event of the decade.
Outrageous headlines guaranteed!

The salacious gossip…

Harlequin Presents invites you to rub shoulders with royalty, sheikhs and glamorous socialites. Step into the decadent playground of the world's rich and famous.
One thing is for sure—royalty has never been so scandalous!

Beginning May 2012

THE PRICE OF ROYAL DUTY—Penny Jordan
THE SHEIKH'S HEIR—Sharon Kendrick
SANTINA'S SCANDALOUS PRINCESS—Kate Hewitt
THE MAN BEHIND THE SCARS—Caitlin Crews
DEFYING THE PRINCE—Sarah Morgan
PRINCESS FROM THE SHADOWS—Maisey Yates
THE GIRL NOBODY WANTED—Lynn Raye Harris
PLAYING THE ROYAL GAME—Carol Marinelli

"Maybe you decided your night with me was so hot that you wanted a repeat of it. I wouldn't blame you if you did."

"I try never to make the same mistake twice, Hassan. Any other suggestions?"

Dark clouds drifted into his mind. "Or our ill-judged liaison has left us with something other than regrets."

She stared at him, because didn't his words make what she was about to tell him even more difficult? "That's the most cold-hearted description I've ever heard," she whispered.

Her lack of denial unsettled him but Hassan kept his nerve. "That's because I am a cold-hearted man, Ella. Be in no doubt of that. And I haven't come here to play guessing games. What is it that you want to say to me?"

"That you're right!" She swallowed as she forced out the bitter truth. She looked into the narrowed black eyes and spoke in a low voice. "I'm having a baby, Hassan."

All about the author...
Sharon Kendrick

SHARON KENDRICK started storytelling at the age of eleven and has never really stopped. She likes to write fast-paced, feel-good romances with heroes who are so sexy they'll make your toes curl!

Born in west London, she now lives in the beautiful city of Winchester—where she can see the cathedral from her window (but only if she stands on tip-toe). She has two children, Celia and Patrick, and her passions include music, books, cooking and eating—and drifting off into wonderful daydreams while she works out new plots!

Visit Sharon at www.sharonkendrick.com.

Other titles by Sharon Kendrick available in ebook

Harlequin Presents®

3041—MONARCH OF THE SANDS
3013—TOO PROUD TO BE BOUGHT
2995—THE FORBIDDEN WIFE

To Max Campbell, for ensuring that
my iPhone plays more than one Beatles song.

CHAPTER ONE

WOULD this damned party never end?

In the softly lit anteroom of his friend's palace, Sheikh Hassan Al Abbas let out an irritated breath and turned to the man standing a few deferential paces away from him.

'Do you think there's any chance I could just slip away and leave them to get on with it, Benedict?' he demanded, knowing only too well how his loyal English aide would respond.

There was a pause. 'Your absence would almost certainly be noticed, Your Highness,' answered Benedict carefully. 'Since you are one of the most esteemed guests present. And furthermore it would offend your oldest friend if he knew that you could not be bothered to stay to wish him happiness on the night of his engagement.'

Hassan's fists clenched against the unaccustomed lounge suit which clothed his hard body, hating the strictures of collar and tie. He wished he was wearing soft and silken robes against his naked skin. That he was galloping free on his horse, with the warm desert wind blowing against his face. 'And what if I believed deep in my heart that such a wish would not only be futile but hypocritical?' he iced back. 'That I think Alex is about to make the biggest mistake of his life?'

'It is often difficult for two men to see eye to eye when it comes to the subject of women,' answered Benedict diplomatically. 'Particularly regarding the subject of marriage.'

'It's not just his choice of fiancée I don't agree with!' Hassan said, unable to contain the frustration which had been growing inside him since his oldest friend, Prince Alessandro Santina, had announced that he was to marry Allegra Jackson. 'Though that is bad enough. Even worse is that he has abandoned the woman to whom he has been betrothed since he was born! A woman of noble birth, who would make a far more suitable bride.'

'Perhaps his love is too strong to be—'

'Love?' interrupted Hassan, and now he could feel the bitter lump which had risen in his throat like a ball of nails. A brief yet undeniable pain clenched at his heart. For didn't he know better than anyone that 'love' was nothing but an illusion which could wreck lives with its seductive power?

'Love is nothing more than a fancy name for lust,' he bit out. 'And a ruler cannot allow himself to be guided by the stir of his loins or the beat of his heart. He must put duty before desire.'

'Yes, Highness,' said Benedict obediently.

Hassan shook his head in disbelief, still unwilling to accept that his high-born friend had let his standards dip so low. 'Did you realise that Alex's future father-in-law is some grubby ex-footballer with a long list of wives and mistresses he has been publicly unfaithful to?'

'I had heard something along those lines, Highness.'

'I cannot believe that he is willing to marry into such a disreputable family as these Jacksons! Did you see the way they were behaving at the ball? It turned my stomach to watch them quaffing champagne as if it was water and making fools of themselves on the dance floor.'

'Highness—'

'This woman Allegra cannot possibly become the wife of a Crown Prince!' Angrily, Hassan slammed the flat of his hand against an adjacent table and its delicate frame juddered beneath the contemptuous force. 'She is a tramp—just like her mother and her sisters! Did you witness the spectacle which brought me seeking refuge in here, when the sister with the voice of a crow stormed the stage and attempted to sing?'

'Yes, Highness, I saw her,' said Benedict softly. 'But the Crown Prince has made up his mind that he will marry Miss Jackson, and I doubt whether even you will be able to change it. And should you not now return to the ballroom before your absence is commented upon?'

But Hassan was not listening—at least, not to his aide. He raised a hand for silence, his ears straining for the whispering of a sound. His body tensed. Had he heard something? Someone? Or had the recent harsh months spent in battle meant that he suspected danger lurking everywhere? Yet he could have sworn that the room had been empty when he'd come searching for an escape.

'Did you hear something?' he questioned as he felt the instinctive pricking of his skin.

'No, Highness. I heard nothing.'

There was a brief silence before Hassan nodded, feeling some of the tension ease from his body as he allowed himself to be reassured by his aide. This might be the worst party in living memory, but at least security was tight. 'Then let us return to this mockery of a reception. Let me see whether I can find anyone tolerably attractive enough to dance with.' He gave a sardonic laugh. 'A woman who is the very antithesis of Allegra Jackson and her vulgar family!'

With this, the two men swept from the softly lit room, while from her hiding place behind a carved chest in a corner of the vast chamber, Ella Jackson wished that she could open her mouth and scream with rage and frustration.

How *dare* he?

Waiting for a few moments to check that he really *had* gone, she stretched limbs which were cramped from sitting still for so long. Greedily, she sucked great gulps of air into her lungs because she'd had to keep holding her breath in case she was discovered. For a moment back then, she'd been sure he was going to find her. And something told her that she was lucky not to have been discovered by that arrogant beast of a man who had been so insulting—not just to Allegra and Izzy, but to the entire Jackson family.

The other man had called him 'Highness'—and judging from the way he'd been calling all the shots, he had certainly *sounded* royal. His voice had been deep and faintly accented—not the kind of voice you heard every day. It had also sounded bossy and proud. Could that have been the powerful sheikh everyone had been banging on about? The groom-to-be's oldest friend, who had been expected at tonight's party and anticipated with the same kind of breathless excitement which might have greeted a movie star?

Uncomfortably, Ella rose to her feet. The beads of her elaborate dress were pressing painfully into her skin and her wild tangle of curls was desperately in need of a session with the hairbrush. She would have to do something drastic to repair her appearance before she thought about returning to the general scrum which was her sister Allegra's engagement party to the Crown Prince of the Santina royal family. Even though she would have happily given a month's salary not to have gone back into that ballroom.

Wasn't it ironic that she had slipped away from the party for precisely the same reason as the sheikh? The moment her sister Izzy had staggered onto the stage to sing, Ella's heart had hit her boots and she'd wanted to curl up and die. She loved Izzy. She *did*—but why did she have such a penchant for making a complete fool of herself? Why sing in public when you had absolutely zero talent?

Ella had slunk into this darkened anteroom and instinct had made her crouch down behind the concealing bulk of the chest when she'd heard the sound of approaching footsteps. There had been the sound of the door quietly clicking shut and then someone uttering a short, terse expletive. And that's when she had heard the damning words of the accented man as he had torn her family to shreds.

Yet hadn't he only been speaking the truth? Her father *did* have a long list of women he'd been intimate with. He had two ex-wives at the last count, and one of those he'd married twice. Plus all the mistresses on the side—some of whom were reported in the newspapers and some whom he'd managed to hush up.

Hadn't her own mother's life been blighted by her hopeless longing for a man who seemed to be incapable of any kind of fidelity? Her sweet, foolish mother, who'd never been able to see any fault in her errant husband, which was why she had been his bride twice over. And why she let him treat her like a complete doormat.

If ever Ella had needed to know how *not* to conduct a relationship, she'd never needed to look any further than the example set by her own parents. And hadn't she vowed that she would never, *ever* let a man make a fool of her like that?

She reached down and picked up her handbag, extracting the wide-toothed comb which was the only implement which could ever come close to taming her soft but wayward curls. Dare she risk putting a brighter light on in here?

Why not? The outrageously opinionated sheikh didn't sound as if he was in any danger of coming back. He was probably subjecting some 'tolerably attractive' woman to a dance. Poor her, Ella thought with a genuine trace of sympathy. Imagine dancing with someone who had an ego as big as his—why there would be barely any room left on the dance floor!

She clicked on a light which illuminated the regal splendour of the vast antechamber and hunted around until she found a mirror recessed in one of the alcoves. Stepping back, she surveyed herself with critical eyes.

Her silver-beaded dress was a little on the short side but it was extremely fashionable—and such a look was essential in Ella's line of work. Her rather flashy clients expected her to reflect their values, to make a statement and not fade quietly into the background. As a party planner catering to the nouveau-riche end of the market, Ella had decided to cash in on her family's notoriety by working for the kind of people who had plenty of money, but very little in the way of generally accepted 'taste.'

She'd quickly learnt the rules. But then, she was a quick learner—it came with the territory of being a survivor, of having lived with scandal and notoriety for most of her life. If a glamour-model bride wanted to arrive at her wedding in a dazzling diamante coach, she expected the woman organising the event to dazzle in a similar way. So dazzle Ella did. She'd got that down to a fine art. With her trademark slash of scarlet lipstick accentuating her wide mouth, she wore the on-trend clothes which so impressed her clients. She turned heads when she needed to.

But all that was for show. She kept the real Ella locked away where no one could find her. Or hurt her. Underneath the dazzling exterior, when she was dressed down and chilled out at home, it was a different story. There she could be the person her family had always teased her for being. Bare of makeup, wearing old jeans and a T-shirt—sometimes with paint underneath her fingernails. She wished she was there right now, instead of having to endure the longest evening of her life. A night she would never have believed could happen.

A member of her family was marrying into one of the Mediterranean's oldest and most revered royal families—and the knives were out. Hadn't she just heard for herself, via the arrogant sheikh, how the entire Jackson clan were being judged and found wanting? Weren't the sly eyes of various members of the press watching every move they made, to report with glee how ill-equipped the Jacksons were to mix with the aristocracy?

Well, Ella would show them. She would show them all. Their cruel comments wouldn't get to her because she wouldn't let them. She bit her lip, for once feeling vulnerable about the charges which were always levelled at her and her siblings. She worked hard for her living—she always had done—and yet her Jackson surname made people pigeonhole her. They thought she just lay around all day, drinking champagne and generally whooping it up, and yet nothing could be further from the truth.

Raking the comb through her red-brown curls, she checked for any stray smudges of mascara and then applied a final, defiant coat of scarlet lipstick.

There.

Her dangling earrings were swaying in a sparkling cascade and even her blue eyeshadow had bits of glitter in it. Her shiny armour was firmly in place and she was ready to face the braying masses. Let anyone *dare* try to patronise her!

The sound of music and chatter grew louder as she clattered along the marble corridor in her new shoes.

In glossy black patent, with towering silver heels which were wonderfully flattering to the legs, they were a fashionista's dream and an orthopaedic surgeon's nightmare. But they made her walk tall and stand straight and tonight she needed that more than anything.

The ballroom was crowded and noisy and Ella's eyes skimmed the dance floor. The place was packed. Royals mingled with minor television stars, and one-time Premier League footballers who'd worked with her dad were propping up the bar. She could see various members of her family partying away with enthusiasm. Rather too *much* enthusiasm. Her father was downing a flute of champagne, her mother hovering nearby with an ever-hopeful smile on her face. Which meant that she was worried he was going to get drunk. Or make a pass at someone young enough to be his daughter.

Please don't let him get drunk, thought Ella. And please don't let him make a pass at someone else's girlfriend. Or wife.

There was her sister Izzy dancing, grinding her hips in a way which made Ella turn away with embarrassment. Knowing there was no point in trying to reason with her wayward sibling, she redirected her gaze to the dance floor. Her heart suddenly beginning to pound as her eyes came to rest on a man whose exotic looks marked him out from everyone else.

She blinked. In a room which wasn't exactly short on the glamour quotient, he drew the eye irresistibly. And yet he looked totally out of place among the glittering throng and she couldn't quite work out why. It wasn't just that he was taller than any other man there or that his muscular body was all hard, honed muscle. He looked *hungry.* Like he hadn't eaten a decent meal in months. Ella's gaze roved over his face. A *cruel* face, she thought with a sudden shiver. His black eyes seemed devoid of emotion and his sensual mouth was curved into a cynical smile as he listened to his blonde dance partner as she lifted her chin to chatter to him.

Ella's heart missed a beat. It was him. Instinct told her so. The man who had been so unspeakably rude about her family when she'd been hiding in the anteroom. The man she had silently cursed as being arrogant and judgemental. And yet now that she'd seen him, she couldn't seem to tear her eyes away from him.

His olive skin gleamed, as if he'd been cast from some precious metal, instead of flesh and blood. She watched as a beautiful redhead brushed past him, saw the way he automatically glanced at her bursting décolletage without missing a beat.

He was danger and sexuality mixed into one potent masculine cocktail—the kind of man most people's mothers would warn you to steer clear of. Ella felt a debilitating kick in her belly, as something deep inside her responded to him. As if on some instinctive level, she had discovered something she hadn't even realised she'd been looking for.

He raised his head then and she saw the way he stilled. The way his black eyes narrowed as he moved his gaze around the ballroom until at last it came to alight on her.

Like a hunter, she thought.

Ella felt as if she had been caught in a dark yet

blinding spotlight. She could feel herself flush—a slow heat which started at the top of her head and seemed to work its way right down to her toes. Had he known she'd been staring at him? Look away, she urged herself furiously. *Look away from him right now.* But she couldn't. It was as if he had cast some powerful spell over her which was making it impossible for her to tear her gaze away.

From across the dance floor, his black eyes grew slightly amused as their overlong eye contact was maintained. A pair of ebony brows were raised at her in arrogant question, and when still she did not move, he bent to whisper something into the blonde's ear.

Ella was aware of the woman turning and glaring at her and of the man with the black eyes beginning to walk towards her. *Run*, she urged herself. Get away from here before it's too late.

But she didn't run. She couldn't. It was as if she'd been turned into a tree and was rooted to the spot. Now he was almost upon her, and his physical presence was so overwhelming that she felt the breath dry in her throat. His shadow moved over her as he approached, enveloping her—and suddenly it was as if every other person in the crowded ballroom had ceased to exist.

There was a pause while he let his eyes rove unashamedly over her face and then her body, just as he'd done when the big-breasted redhead had passed him by.

'Have we met somewhere before?' he questioned.

Ella didn't have to hear his deep, accented voice to know that she had been right. It *was* him. The opinionated man who'd been so rude about her family. She'd already decided that he was proud and arrogant, but she hadn't expected this level of charisma. Nor for him to have such an overwhelming effect on her that she could barely think straight. And she needed to think straight. Now was not the time to demonstrate that her tingling body seemed to have taken on a greedy life of its own. All she needed was to remember his unforgettable insults.

'Not until now,' she said, injecting a noncommittal note into her voice and hoping it sounded convincing.

Hassan's eyes flicked over her, interested at the play of emotions on the Madonna-like oval of her face. She had been staring at him as if she'd like to rip his clothes off with her teeth! Not an uncommon reaction from a woman, it was true—and she was pretty enough for him to have given the idea a moment's consideration. But her initial hungry look had been replaced by one of wariness and suspicion. He felt the faint prickle of hostility emanating from her, and *that* was novel enough to arouse his interest.

'Are you sure about that?' he murmured.

She thought how incredibly well he spoke English, despite the sexily accented voice. It seemed to whisper over her skin with its velvet caress, and inexplicably she started wondering what it would be like to have that voice murmur sweet nothings in her ear. 'Positive,' she replied coolly.

'Yet you were staring at me as if you knew me.'

'Aren't you used to women staring at you, then?' she questioned innocently.

'No, never happened to me before,' he drawled sardonically, wondering what was making her blow so hot and cold. He looked at the provocative scarlet gleam of her lips and felt a sudden rush of desire. 'What's your name?'

Ella wished that her breasts would stop tingling and likewise the molten throb of lust deep in her belly. She didn't want to feel like this about a man who had talked about her family in a way which had made them all sound like some sort of *gutter animals.* She stared at him, defying him to contradict her. 'My name is… Cinderella.'

Hassan gave a slow smile. 'Is it now?' So she wanted to play, did she? Well, that was fine by him. He liked games—particularly of the flirty, sexual nature. And particularly with nubile young women with glossy, red lips and firm bodies which had been poured into a shiny silver dress which emphasised their every willowy curve. As a child, the only female role models he'd known had been servants and as an adult he had discovered that women were usually predatory and nearly always beddable.

He felt the sudden beat of anticipation as he looked at her. 'Then I think the fairy tale must have just come true, Cinderella,' he said. 'Because you've just met your prince.'

It was the corniest line Ella had ever heard and yet, somehow, it worked. For some insane reason it made her want to smile—a little I'm-so-pleased-with-myself sort of smile to accompany the embarrassing rise of colour to her cheeks.

But she didn't fall for meaningless chat-up lines, did she? Hadn't she learnt—from the humiliating example set by her own father—that men spent their lives saying things to women that they didn't mean? And hadn't she vowed never to become one of those women who drank up worthless compliments and then let their hearts get broken as a result?

Drawing back her shoulders, she stared at the exotic-looking man, pleased that she'd worn such ridiculously high heels which meant that their eyes were almost on a level. 'So you're a real live prince, are you?'

'Indeed I am.' For a moment, Hassan felt a flicker of impatience, acknowledging his own obstinacy. He didn't like being recognised for his royal blood and yet he found it faintly irritating when his regal status was not alluded to. He wasn't expecting her to curtsey—which was a good thing, since she clearly had no intention of doing so!—but a little deference surely wouldn't have gone amiss? Surely she could have allowed a small amount of awe to creep into an English accent which he found oddly difficult to place. 'In fact, I am a sheikh,' he expanded proudly. 'My name is Hassan, and I am a prince of the desert.'

'Wow!'

Hassan's eyes narrowed. Was that *sarcasm* he had heard tingeing her voice? Surely not. People were always impressed by his sheikhdom, indeed being ravished by a sheikh seemed to be the number-one sexual fantasy among most of the Western women he met. Yet the uncertainty of her response fired his blood into a slow, pulsing heat. The cat-like slant of her blue eyes was very appealing and he felt another kick of lust as he imagined those eyes growing opaque in time to the powerful thrust of his body. He swallowed, for his groin had grown exquisitely hard in conjunction with his thoughts.

'And now I think we are supposed to dance,' he said unevenly. Slowly, he allowed his gaze to travel all the way down her legs to where her feet were encased in a pair of toweringly high stilettos. 'Before you run off as the clock strikes midnight, and leave one of those gravity-defying and very sexy shoes behind.'

Ella's heart hammered. Of course she *knew* the shoes were sexy—you didn't wear heels this high because they were comfortable. But it came as something of a shock to hear him come right out and say so like that. There was something very blatant about his remark. It made her feel…*weird*…. As if she was something she wasn't. As if she'd worn them so that an arrogant sheikh might look at her legs with unashamed appraisal. And she had certainly not done that.

Every instinct she possessed was screaming out to her to get away from him. But even as the adrenalin pumped around her body, wasn't there a contrary instinct urging her to do precisely the opposite? Didn't she have some insane desire for him to take her into his arms and pull her against his powerful body to see whether he felt as good as he looked?

'I'm not really that into dancing,' she said truthfully.

'Ah, but that's because you've never danced with me,' he drawled as he took her by the hand and led her onto the dance floor. 'Once you have, you'll change your mind. You'll become an instant convert, believe me.'

Ella swallowed. What an arrogant boast to make! Now was the moment for her to wrench her hand away from the firm grip of his fingers and walk away from him and these confused emotions she was experiencing.

So why was she letting him lead her to a spot where the overhanging chandeliers spilled their fractured diamond spangles onto the glossy dance floor? Because she liked his touch, that was why. It was that simple and that complex and it was doing strange things to her. Making her feel light-headed and excited. Making her heart race as if she had just endured an hour's hard workout at the gym.

She felt a brief flash of shame but still she didn't move. And she knew she was about to betray her family by dancing with a man who despised them.

Without warning, Hassan took her into his arms and his presence enveloped her, just as his shadow had done earlier. His body felt as warm and as hard as she'd imagined and she moved closer to him, as his hands splayed possessively across her back.

Remember all those things he said about your family, she reminded herself dazedly. About Izzy sounding like a crow and them all being nothing but tramps.

And yet it was difficult to remember the insults when he was holding her in his arms like this. Difficult to do anything other than melt against him.

'You smell beautiful,' he murmured. 'Of summer meadows in the sun.'

With an effort, Ella lifted her head to stare at the proud jut of his jaw. 'What do sheikhs know of summer meadows?'

'Plenty. When I was a boy, I used to come and visit Alex and sometimes we would go to England, to play the polo at which we both excelled. It was there that I learned that the smell of newly mown grass was one of the most seductive smells in the world.' He smiled against her hair. Particularly if there was a nubile and willing female lying in it, with most of her clothes undone.

Ella could now feel the gentle caress of his fingertips on her bare skin and she knew she had to stop this before it went any further. Before his sexy voice and sure touch made her do anything else she regretted. Turning her face up, she flashed him a smile which was completely insincere. 'You must have been amazed to find someone *tolerably attractive* to dance with among all these women here tonight,' she observed. 'Should I be flattered?'

Hassan frowned at the unexpected change of topic, some subtle emphasis in her words nudging at a faint memory. 'Perhaps you should.' He moved his hand to allow his fingers to tangle briefly in the spill of curls which danced around at the base of her waist. 'Though I imagine that flattery is something you're quite used to.'

The easy compliment slipped off his tongue and it helped fuel her indignation. Ella wriggled a little in his arms. 'Are you always this predictable when you talk to women?'

'Predictable? You want me to be a little more original, do you, Cinderella?' he questioned, feeling the provocative thrust of her beaded breasts pressing into his chest. 'But that would be exceedingly difficult with someone who looks like you. What can I tell you that countless men haven't said before? You must be bored with hearing that your eyes are the blue of a summer sky. Or that your hair is so lustrous that if I moved a little closer, I'd swear I'd be able to see my face in its reflection.'

He positioned his head as if he intended to do just that, but instead he found that his eyes were closing and that he was breathing her in and pulling her against his body. And that suddenly he wanted her very much. It had been, he realised achingly, a long time since he'd held a woman in his arms. Particularly a woman who sent out messages as conflicting as this one…

Ella felt his arms tighten around her and was appalled at how much she wanted to sink further into that embrace. To feel the beat of his heart and to listen to those admiring comments which he probably said to every woman and which meant precisely nothing.

'Hassan,' she said, realising how thready her voice sounded. But why wouldn't it sound like that when he had just splayed his hands so proprietarily over her back? She was wearing a dress which left a lot of skin on show. Skin to which he now had access. She felt the almost imperceptible caress of his fingers and she shivered with a strange kind longing. She had to stop this.

'Or the most beautiful pair of lips I've ever seen. Tell me, does that lipstick come off when a man kisses you and does it taste of roses, or berries?'

'Hassan,' she said again, more weakly this time.

'Mmm? I like it when you say my name. Say it again. Say it as if you want to ask me a big, big favour and let me see if I can guess what that favour might be.'

With an effort, she ignored the shockingly erotic

command and pulled away from him so that she could see his reaction. 'What do you think of the bride-to-be?'

A look of displeasure crossed his face as the sensual mood was broken by her unexpected question. For a moment back then, he'd almost forgotten where he was—and he did not care to be reminded. 'I don't think you want to know,' he said, an unmistakable note of finality in his voice warning her that he did not wish to pursue the topic.

'Oh, but I do,' argued Ella. 'I'm fascinated to hear your opinion. I'm sure it'll be really enlightening.'

He drew back. She was enchanting in her own way, but he thought that she was in danger of overstepping the mark. Didn't she realise that if he wanted a subject closed, then it was closed? Immediately. And that persisting with her girlie questionnaire to test out his views on marriage—which was clearly what this was all about—would put a complete dampener on the rest of the evening? Because if he told her the truth—that marriage was not for him—wouldn't her beautiful scarlet lips inevitably crumple with disappointment?

He wanted to dance with her, to feel the softness of her skin and the press of her flesh against his. If she continued to please him, then he might later take her to his bed, but she must quickly learn that his word was law.

'I think that the less said about the bride-to-be, the better, don't you?' he drawled dismissively.

'No, I don't, actually.' Ella saw the spark of warning glittering in the depths of his black eyes and a sudden, heady power infused her. Was he so spoiled that he was used to people just falling in with his wishes every time he snapped his fingers? Yes, he probably was. She recalled the words of his aide. The smarmy way he had tried to talk him round. Ugh! She leaned forward, her voice probably not as low as it should have been but her rage was so profound that she didn't care. 'But then you've probably exhausted the topic since you've already said quite a few nasty things about Allegra, haven't you?'

He stiffened. 'I *beg* your pardon?'

He had relaxed his hold on her and Ella took the opportunity to step away from the distraction of his touch, staring fearlessly into the ebony glitter of his eyes. 'You heard me,' she said. 'But perhaps you're suffering from some sort of short-term memory loss and need me to remind you of the things you said. Shall I do that?'

'What the hell are you talking about?'

Ella began to count the facts off against her fingers. 'Let's see, you think she's highly unsuitable and that Alex shouldn't be marrying her. Didn't you describe her as a "tramp"—just like her mother and sisters? And didn't you say that you considered the whole Jackson family far too "vulgar" ever to be related to the Crown Prince of Santina?'

'Where the hell did you hear all this?' he demanded.

'I notice that you don't deny it!' she accused, her voice growing louder as several of the other dancers turned their heads to see what was going on. She could see the dawning light of recognition in his eyes and she leapt in for the final thrust, a fierce protectiveness sweeping over her as she thought of her wayward family. 'You delivered your damning verdict on people you have never met, didn't you? And then you left to find someone "tolerably attractive" to dance with. And that someone just happened to be me!'

There was a split second of a pause before his eyes narrowed as he looked at her. 'You're one of the Jacksons?' he guessed.

'Oh, bravo, *Sheikh* Hassan! *Prince of the desert!* It took you long enough to work it out, didn't it? Yes, I'm one of the Jacksons!'

Resisting the desire to show her just how speedy his responses could be, he glared at her. 'You were eavesdropping in the anteroom!'

'And if I was?'

'Eavesdropping!' he repeated contemptuously. A slow anger began to build inside him as he met the defiant light in her blue eyes. But in truth, he was furious with himself for not having followed his own instincts. He had *thought* that he'd heard something, and yet he had allowed himself to be convinced otherwise. And wasn't that lazy and dangerous behaviour from a king, especially one who had just left behind a war zone? Was he getting complacent now that he was away from the battlefields?

He lowered his voice to an angry hiss. 'That's exactly the kind of vulgar attitude I would have expected from a family such as yours, and one which completely vindicates my belief about your general unsuitability to be mixing in royal circles. I rest my case.'

It wasn't so much the hateful things he was saying which made Ella's blood boil, but the sanctimonious way he was saying them. As if *he* was in the right and she was in the wrong! As if he was allowed to say what he pleased and there wasn't a thing she could do about it. Her blood was pounding in her veins as she felt her rage rise, and an odd kind of hurt and frustration come bubbling to the surface.

People were staring at them quite openly now, but she didn't care.

'Unsuitability?' she declared. 'I'll show you unsuitability if you want!' Almost without thinking, she grabbed a glass of champagne from a passing waitress and tossed it over his dark, mocking face before turning to push her way through the throng of open-mouthed spectators.

CHAPTER TWO

FOR a moment Hassan was frozen into shocked immobility, scarcely able to believe what had just happened. The impudent minx of a Jackson girl had thrown champagne over him!

Angrily, he wiped both cheeks, aware that people were staring at him, their voices beginning to rise in excited chatter above the brief, stunned silence which had followed their very public row. But he barely paid them any attention. He was too busy watching the tottering sway of 'Cinderella' Jackson's silver-clad bottom as she moved through the ballroom, as swiftly as her ridiculously high heels would allow.

He could see his bodyguard fixing him with a questioning look, as if seeking permission to go after her and give her a crash course in royal protocol. But Hassan gave a decisive shake of his head as a cold realisation crept over him.

How dare she humiliate him in such a way? And in *public*! Why, if a man in his own country had done such a thing, he would have been thrown immediately into the city jail!

His mouth hardening into a grim line, he began to follow her, his long stride quickly covering the distance between them. Now he was close enough to hear the clatter of her high heels on the marble floor and see the gleam of light as it highlighted the curve of her silver-beaded bottom. He saw her glance over her shoulder, her blue eyes widening when she saw him behind her, and a brief sensation of anticipation rippled over his skin as she increased her speed.

Silently, he pursued her, pleased when she briefly hesitated between two corridors—one wide and one narrow. She wouldn't have a clue where she was going, he thought with satisfaction, whereas he knew well the labyrinth network of passageways which comprised the Santina palace. Hadn't he and Alex played hide-and-seek in them often enough when they were children?

She chose the narrower passage and he continued to shadow her, knowing that he could easily have caught up with her there and then but he was enjoying the thrill of the chase too much to want to end it. It was like being back in battle, his senses honed and heightened as he pursued his quarry….

Only when the main body of the palace had retreated and the corridors were bare of servants did he surge forward. She whirled round as he backed her into a corner, her breath coming in short little pants. Her abundant curls were spilling down over the silver dress, one thigh was pushed forward as if to showcase its honed perfection, and he thought that he had never seen a woman look so wild and so wanton.

'Got you,' he said, his voice a triumphant murmur, but he didn't touch her.

Ella stared at him, her heart pounding so hard that it felt as if it was about to leap out of her chest. She was hot and out of breath. Running in these heels had been a stupid thing to try to do because her feet now felt as if they were on fire. What had possessed her to react like that? To dare to chuck a drink over a man who was now towering above her looking like the devil incarnate, a patch of his pristine white shirt clinging wetly to his chest. A man who was different from every other man she'd ever met. Well, she had done it, and now she just had to keep her nerve.

'You don't scare me!' she blurted out, but she wondered how convincing her words were as she met emptiness of his eyes.

'Don't I?' Hassan leaned in a little. 'Then maybe I need to try a little harder. Most people would be pretty scared of my reaction if they'd done what you've just done.' He observed her rapid breathing which was causing the silver beads over her breasts to shimmer in a provocative sway. And suddenly it was difficult to remember just why he was so angry. He swallowed, so unbearably turned on that for a moment he could not speak. 'That was some scene you created back there.'

Ella told herself that she ought to tread carefully. That she was dealing with someone who had danger written all over him. Someone who she, with her laughable lack of experience, didn't have a clue how to deal with. The voice of reason was telling her to try to make it right between them, yet the apology she knew she really ought to make stayed stubbornly unspoken. For how could she forget those harsh things he'd said?

'Who cares about a scene?' she questioned stubbornly.

He met the defiance in her ice-blue eyes. 'Clearly

you don't, but then you don't have any reputation to wreck, do you?'

Actually, she *did.* She'd worked hard to build her own business and she survived on the income it provided. But the irony was that causing a scene with the sheikh was likely to bring new customers flocking to her, instead of taking their custom elsewhere. The fact that she was even *mixing* with royals would be great publicity. A bit of scandal never seemed to affect *her* client base. Hadn't she noticed a definite growth in business whenever her father's face was splashed all over the papers, no matter how dodgy the story? 'And you do, I suppose?'

'Of course I do!' he snapped. 'I am the ruler of a desert kingdom and my word is law. In fact, I *make* the laws.'

'Wow! Mr. Powerful,' she mocked.

Her insolence was turning him on almost as much as it was infuriating him. He felt a muscle working in his cheek and an even more insistent throbbing at his groin. 'And I have people who look up to me who will not enjoy reading that their king had champagne flung at him by a brazen English nobody.'

'I should have thought that people would have been used to your *flings* by now!' she returned, and for one brief moment she thought she saw the edges of his lips tilt in the beginning of a smile. But it quickly disappeared and so did her small moment of triumph as she reminded herself that this man was the enemy. 'Anyway, you should have thought about that before you started laying into my family.'

'By telling the truth, you mean?'

'It's not—'

'Oh, please, spare me the empty defence!' His eyes took on a look of challenge. 'You're denying that your father is no stranger to the bankruptcy court? Or that your sister's awful singing brought the house down, but not in a good way? Or that the Crown Prince has dumped his long-term girlfriend and fiancée in order to marry your other sister?'

Ella gritted her teeth. 'If only there was another waitress nearby, I'd happily upend *another* drink all over you!'

'Would you now?' He tilted his head to one side and studied her. 'And do you make a habit of resorting to playground tactics?'

'Only if I'm forced to deal with the class bully!' Ella stared at him with growing bewilderment. Why did she feel this overpowering sense of *frustration* which was making her want to pummel her fists against the solid wall of his chest? 'Actually, I've never done anything like that before.'

'No? You just thought you'd make an exception for me, did you?' He stared at her, wanting to crush her rosy lips beneath his. Wanting more than that. Wanting to feel the soft surrender of her body as it gave itself up to the hard dominance of his own. 'I wonder why?'

The arrogant flick of his gaze made her skin grow heated. 'Because you're overbearing, overopinionated and ridiculously traditional? Could that give you some sort of clue? You spout such outdated and macho comments that it's obviously made me react to you in an uncharacteristically primitive way!' Raking her fingers back through the wayward spill of her curls, she glared at him. 'And you obviously haven't got a clue what the modern world is like.'

His eyes narrowed. 'You think that I am a stranger to the modern world?'

Suddenly, Ella wasn't sure what she thought. Not any more. Not when he was staring at her so intently and every cell in her body was responding to that black-eyed scrutiny. Her senses seemed to be short-circuiting her brain, but there was one thing she was certain of. He'd just lumped her in with the rest of her family and he seemed stubbornly unrepentant about doing it. Maybe it was time he discovered how it felt to be treated as if you were simply a stereotype, instead of an individual.

She met the challenge in his eyes with one of her own. 'Yes, I think you're a stranger to the modern world! How can you not be? How can you know how most people live if you're stuck in some remote desert country where you probably travel round by camel and sleep in a tent?'

For a moment Hassan could scarcely believe his ears. *Camel?* It was true that his most recent months had been spent on horseback as he had battled to settle the long-running dispute on the borders of his country. But although much in his life involved the ancient and the traditional, he had also insisted on embracing every new technology, for he recognised that there could be no real progress without it. He thought about his fleet of cars, the state-of-the-art aircraft and the engineers he employed to search for ever more eco-friendly alternative travel.

'Now you insult my land,' he observed furiously. 'And thus my honour.'

'As you did mine!'

He met the rebellious gleam in her blue eyes. 'I said nothing which isn't true. Whereas you have just passed judgement on my homeland without knowing a single thing about it.'

'Well, that's tough. Deal with it. And now, if you wouldn't mind stepping out of the way, I'd like to leave.'

Hassan tensed. Was it her continuing defiance which made something inside him tighten? Something which had been tightening ever since he'd first started dancing with her and felt her soft and fragrant body in his arms.

Women never answered him back like this. They usually went out of their way to accommodate him. They didn't hurl champagne at him and then storm away, wiggling their silver bottom in a provocative movement which was designed to ensnare his fast-hardening body. For all her professed disdain of him and all he stood for, there was an undeniable sexual charge sparking through the air between them. It had been there from the outset and nothing they'd said or done had diminished it. He could read her hunger in the darkening of her eyes and in the flagrant thrust of her nipples as they pushed against the tiny silver beads of her dress.

He felt urgent sexual desire fire him up, heating his blood with its insistent throb. He'd barely been a week back from battle when he had flown here to Alex's party and the contrast between this glittering event and the months of arid hardship could not have been greater.

Warfare put many pressures on a man and perhaps the greatest of those was the absence of sex. For so long now he had sublimated his fierce sexual appetite in battle that it had become almost habitual. In some ways he welcomed it, for not only did it channel his energy into fighting, it also made him feel powerful. It gave him strength to know that he could subdue the weaknesses of the flesh. Yet how could he have forgotten what it felt like to be in thrall to his senses? And how could he not but thank a fate which had conspired to put him alone with a beautiful and eager young woman?

He looked around. The corridor was empty and bare of staff. Should he take her here and risk discovery? Or simply give her a taste of what would inevitably follow—the teasing brush of his lips over hers, the butterfly caress of his fingers over her jewel-covered breasts?

Yet he recognised that this tumble-haired brunette was a challenge, and that only fuelled his hunger, for he loved to conquer and to tame. That was his default mechanism. A way of inflicting control onto a life which had been filled with chaos.

Now that his anger had dissipated, there remained only desire. He remembered her defiance and the way she had struck him and his heart began to thunder. How it would please him to see her subdued. To hear her begging him to enter her, her fiery spirit temporarily silenced by her hunger for him!

His eyes were drawn downwards to see the way

she had wriggled a restless-looking foot and he gave a slow smile, for he could read women as well as he could read his beloved falcons when he raced them over the desert skies.

'Your feet are aching,' he observed softly.

Ella's eyes widened, momentarily disarmed by the lazy question in his. Had he read her mind? And what was it about this quiet corner of the palace which made her feel as if they had been suddenly cloaked in a quiet intimacy, so that she responded to him frankly? 'My shoes are killing me,' she admitted.

'Then take them off. Isn't that what Cinderella is supposed to do?'

The words were faintly erotic and Ella opened her mouth to protest, but when she thought about it, why not? Loads of women shed their shoes at parties. Some even secreted a pair of pumps in their bag. She made as if to bend but before she could move Hassan was there before her, crouching down to slide off both her high heels with a dexterity which made her think he might have done that kind of thing before. Briefly, he ran a thumb across her cramped toes and they gave an appreciative little wriggle before he put them down to meet the delicious coolness of the marble floor.

He straightened up, his black eyes mocking as they looked at her. 'Better?'

Ella nodded. Sure, her feet now felt comfortable and free, but stupidly she was missing his touch. Because hadn't it felt like some kind of delicious intimacy to have the sheikh's fingers on her toes? She forced a smile.

'Much better,' she said.

He handed her the shoes. 'Are you heading back to the party?'

Hooking her fingers through the glittery slingbacks, she shook her head. She couldn't possibly go back now, and not just because she had left the ballroom in such dramatic circumstances. She just couldn't face any more of this wretched partying, supposedly celebrating an engagement which nobody seemed happy about. Except for the happy couple, presumably.

'No. I think I'll call it a night. I need to organise a car to get back to my hotel.'

'I'll walk you back to the main entrance.'

Ella's heart raced as fear and desire fused into a molten ache at the base of her belly. It was something to do with the way he was looking at her, her sudden awareness of how close he was. Close enough for her to be able to inhale his distinctly masculine scent, just as he'd done on the dance floor. And to remember him sliding the shoes from her feet like some old-fashioned fairy tale, in reverse. Because wasn't the prince supposed to put the shoe *on*? She felt the rapid thunder of her heart. 'No, honestly. I'll be fine.'

His eyes narrowed. 'You know where you're going, do you?'

For the first time she became aware of her surroundings, of the dim silence of the cool corridor, in a network of passageways which all seemed to look exactly the same. She suddenly realised that there were no sounds of revelry drifting towards them and that they must be miles away from the other guests. But then she'd run like the wind, hadn't she? Running to escape him wearing too-high heels which explained her aching feet and why she now found herself in some unknown corner of a strange palace.

Should she brazen it out? Tell him that she'd find her own way back and she didn't need his help, thank you very much? That would be the most sensible thing. To walk away with her pride intact, and with some sort of uneasy truce having been reached between them. 'I'll be fine.'

'Are you sure? It's a bit of a maze. And I'd hate to think of you wandering around in circles for hours.'

'But a maze which you can negotiate with the ease of a born navigator, I suppose?'

He shrugged his shoulders. 'As it happens, I do have a superb sense of direction, but I also happen to know the palace well. I used to spend a lot of time here with Alex when we were children.'

Ella's fingers tightened around the straps of her shoes. It was strange to imagine this towering man with the cruel face ever having been a child. Had he told her that to emphasise his own royal credentials, reinforcing the fact that *her* family were simply arriviste social climbers?

Yet as she met the mockery in his black eyes, she realised that maybe she should do the grown-up thing and accept his offer. The last thing she wanted was to spend hours walking around this cavernous place and wandering into some part of the palace which was out of bounds.

She need never see him again—except, presumably, at the wedding, when her sister would marry his friend. And surely it would be better to part on cordial terms, particularly after she'd thrown champagne all over him. In fact, it was surprising and rather reassuring that he seemed to have forgotten all about that.

This time her smile was wider, even if it didn't feel exactly joyful. But then *joy* wasn't a word you really associated with a man whose eyes were so hard and so black they looked as if they'd been made from some rare, cold stone. 'In that case, yes, please. I wouldn't mind being pointed in the right direction.'

Hassan allowed a brief smile to curve the edges of his lips. 'Let's go,' he said softly, knowing instantly the route he was about to take.

They made no sound as they moved through the high-ceilinged passage, but Ella was so aware of him that she didn't take in any of the spectacular surroundings. For once, the ornate decor was completely overshadowed by Hassan himself. Without the added inches of her heels, his height and his breadth were almost intimidating. Did he always dominate his surroundings and the people in them? she wondered.

His question broke into her muddled thoughts. 'How long are you staying on the island?'

'I'm flying back to London tomorrow.'

'After lunch?'

Ella shrugged, dreading the thought of yet another formal meal while people looked down their noses at her and her family. She'd been hoping to escape and slip back to England straight after breakfast but from what she understood attendance at the lunch seemed to be mandatory. She was quickly learning that you weren't allowed to say no to royals. 'Yes.'

Hearing the note of heavy resignation in her voice, Hassan glanced down at her. She wasn't doing anything he had expected her to do. He'd expected a little more gratitude that he'd forgiven her for her shocking display of temper, and the seductive removal of her shoes would usually have guaranteed that by now she'd be glancing up at him from beneath her lashes and flirting like crazy. But she was doing no such thing. Instead her gaze seemed fixed firmly ahead of her, like a runner who had their eyes on the finish line. Like someone longing to reach their destination.

Was she?

Or was she just trying to dampen down the desire which had been so apparent since they'd first set eyes on each other? He let his eyes linger on her body as she moved. The shimmer of her silver dress was enhancing her willowy frame and the thick gleam of her dark hair made him want to run his fingers through it. And somehow her bare toes, with their gleam of silver polish, were much sexier without the stilt-like shoes he'd just removed. He felt a renewed stab of lust.

'So would you like a glass of champagne before you leave?' he questioned. 'Or is that just asking for trouble?'

'Champagne?' It was the hint of unexpected humour in his voice which made her waver, until she reminded herself of her dramatic exit from the ballroom. She stared up at him, her hair shimmying around her face. 'But I don't want to go back to the party.'

'I know. But since we're right by my own suite, I thought you might like to see it.' His lips curved into a smile. 'Especially as it happens to contain some fabulous paintings.'

It was ironic that he seemed unwittingly to have hit

on the one thing designed to make her heart beat faster and yet Ella's one feeling was one of disappointment. It seemed that all men were predictably similar, whether they were desert princes or hedge fund managers. 'As in, "Come up and see my etchings," I suppose?' she questioned sarcastically. 'Gosh, you really *do* need to take a refresher course when you're trying to chat up a woman!'

'I had no idea that I was dealing with such an expert in chat-up lines,' he murmured. 'Or perhaps you just don't like beautiful paintings?'

She heard the subtle put-down. There was that judgement of his all over again. Did he think she was too common to appreciate anything of beauty, that a Jackson would only ever enjoy some mindless pap on TV, or flicking through an undemanding glossy magazine? The anger which she'd thought had been extinguished now began to simmer once more. But infuriatingly, it was manifesting itself in the prickle of her breasts and a soft, melting feeling at the fork of her thighs. It was making her throat dry just to look at him, and her heart fluttered madly. 'Or perhaps I just don't like strange men coming on to me with sexual innuendo?'

'Ah, Cinders, Cinders,' he mocked as he watched the battle between her provocative words and her blossoming body. And wasn't it echoing the same battle which was taking place in his own? 'I was simply talking about art, yet all you seem to want to talk about is sex. And just what *is* your real name, by the way?'

'It's Ella,' she said, her head spinning. 'And will you

please stop twisting everything I say? I *don't* want to talk about sex!'

'Neither do I,' he agreed unexpectedly. 'Since talking about it is a complete waste of time.'

Before she properly realised what he was going to do, he had pulled her into his arms. Pulled her right up close to his aroused body and, with a thrill of shocked recognition, she was letting him. An urgent kind of hunger overwhelmed her as she felt the weight of his hands at her back. The touch of his fingers on her bare skin was as electric as it had been on the dance floor and it had precisely the same sizzling effect on her. Only this time they weren't in a crowd with the curious eyes of thc other dancers on them. This time they were dangerously alone.

She opened her mouth to say something but by then his curiously empty eyes had begun to blaze into life as he lowered his head towards her. And then it was too late.

His lips came down to meet hers and Ella's mouth opened of its own volition, and she found herself unwillingly lost in the most sensational kiss of her life.

CHAPTER THREE

ELLA swayed as Hassan kissed her, his arms tightening around her so that every hard sinew of his powerful frame seemed to be imprinted indelibly on her body. She could feel the pricking of her breasts and their sudden aching heaviness as they pressed against him. And she could feel the coiling heat which was building inside her, pooling in an erotic, silken warmth at the juncture of her thighs.

The thunder of her heart played a backing-track as his lips explored hers and she sank against him. Yet even as his tongue slid inside her mouth and her eyelids fluttered to a close she knew that something wasn't right. Through a haze, she tried to remember just what that something was, but her greedy body seemed intent on pushing all sane thoughts from her mind. The blood pooling in her breasts and at her groin was denying her brain the vital fuel it needed in order to think clearly. But how could she think clearly when she was feeling like *this*?

She gasped as Hassan caught hold of her breast, his big hand splaying with arrogant possession over its hardening swell. Against the finely beaded surface, he teased the already-aching nipple with his finger, and at that split second she remembered the source of her discomfort.

She hated him.

And he hated her.

He was supposed to be showing her the way out of the palace…and instead he had her pressed up against some cool palace wall where he seemed intent on having hot and urgent sex with her.

So why wasn't she pushing him away and professing outrage at his seduction? Why was she winding the arm which wasn't holding her shoes around his neck and breathing urgent little sounds of encouragement?

Because she'd never felt like this before.

Never imagined that a woman could feel like this when a man kissed her. As if this was what her body had been invented for. Her one previous sexual experience now just seemed a mockingly bland rehearsal for this rapid awakening which was making her blood fizz.

But it was wrong. It was *very, very* wrong.

'Hassan.' With an effort, she tore her mouth away from his as her high heels nearly slipped from her fingers onto the floor. 'This is…absolutely…*crazy*….' She thought how weak her voice sounded. As if he had somehow sapped all her strength and resolve.

'Don't break the spell, Cinderella,' he warned unsteadily, pushing open the door to his suite. Pulling her inside, he kicked the door shut, before taking her into his arms and beginning to kiss her again, as if that might obliterate any objections she might have.

And it was working, wasn't it? It didn't seem to matter that she was in the bedroom of a man who was a virtual stranger—a dark and empty-eyed sheikh who had spoken about her family with the cruel lash of his tongue. Such was his skill that he melted away every single doubt beneath the practised caress of his lips. His hands stroked their way down over her body as he kissed her, until her nerve endings were raw with desire and she was moving restlessly in his arms.

Her skin felt heated, her body on fire. She groaned when he cupped her breast again, his thumb brushing negligently against the bead-covered nipple. Why couldn't he touch her bare skin instead, she wondered distractedly when, as if he'd read her thoughts again, he reached out and peeled down the flimsy bodice of her dress.

He leaned back a little to survey her, the way people did in art galleries when they wanted to get a better look at a painting. His eyes seemed to devour her breasts and she felt the skin tighten and tingle beneath that fierce black scrutiny.

'Do you always go braless?' he questioned unsteadily.

She wanted to tell him that the fashionable dress had made the wearing of a bra impossible but somehow the words seemed to have lodged in her throat.

'But then again, why would you ever cover up anything so beautiful as these pert little breasts?' he continued as he grazed a lazy thumb over one hardening nub. 'I like the fact that they are so instantly accessible. That they are within easy reach of the curl of my tongue.'

She wanted to protest at the outrageous mastery of his words but he leaned forward to suckle a taut nipple and the corresponding shaft of desire made her body shudder helplessly.

She could see the erotic contrast of his black head against her pale skin and could feel his tongue licking sensual pathways over the diamond-hard nub. And suddenly, the pleasure almost became too intense to bear. She felt her knees begin to sag and he responded by bending down to curl his arm beneath them to pick her up. He carried her across the glittering gilded room towards an arch beyond which she could see a massive, canopied bed. And the reality of what was about to happen hit home.

'Hassan?'

'That's my name.'

His teasing words momentarily distracted her. But not nearly as much as the warmth of his fingers as they pressed against her bare flesh. 'We…we shouldn't be doing this.'

'Shouldn't we? You don't sound very certain.'

That's because she wasn't. She'd never been carried by a man before and it was making her feel intensely *feminine.* As if for the first time in her life, she'd found someone strong enough to protect her. Her loosened dress was flapping against her bare breasts and she looked up to find his black eyes burning into her as if she was the most beautiful thing he'd ever seen. She had never felt quite so desired, nor so deliciously compliant.

He put her down on the bed and she lay there watching as he shrugged off his jacket and let it fall to the floor. His tie followed, and then his silk shirt. Shoes and socks were efficiently disposed of and then his hand moved to the belt of his trousers, gingerly easing them down over his formidable erection. Completely absorbed by what was happening, Ella stared at him, unable to tear her eyes away from his magnificent body. Surely she should have felt shy at such a careless striptease, but she didn't feel a bit shy. Was that because he knew that his hard, honed body was the closest thing to perfection she had ever seen?

He moved to the bed, his face a dark mask as he bent over her, his fingers moving to find the zip of her dress. But the zip seemed to have been jammed by some errant beads and when he tugged at it, the whole thing split, sending silver beads spilling all around them, some rolling from the bed and others cascading onto the floor. Ella heard someone laugh and realised that someone was her, and that her arms were reaching up to him and pulling him down to her.

He gave an unsteady laugh. 'So your sexual appetite matches your temper, does it, Cinders?'

'Does yours?' she murmured back, completely forgetting her abysmal track record with men as she felt the brush of his lips over her shoulder.

Her provocative reply fired him up even more. Hassan had never felt quite so out of control before, knowing that what he was about to do was sheer madness and yet somehow powerless to stop himself. Because hadn't he denied himself the comfort of a woman for too long? He had forgotten how it felt to touch silken skin, and the sweet contrast between the hard male body and its yielding female counterpart.

Yet there were a hundred women more suitable as

lovers than she. Women back in that ballroom who had plenty of aristocratic credentials. Who knew how to behave and how not to behave. Who would never have doused him in champagne and then submitted to him so easily. He should go back right now. Renounce this insolent Jackson while he still had the strength left in him to do so.

But now her milky thighs were spreading wide, silently urging him into their secret, molten depths, and Hassan knew that it was too late. With fingers which weren't quite steady, he reached for a condom. Everything he wanted at that moment was centred on this woman and all he had to do was push his hard flesh into her silken sweetness to find that elusive peace.

Unable to wait any longer, he slithered her skimpy lace panties down, tossing them away before moving over her and positioning himself against her quivering heat. With an urgent moan he entered her, moving deep into her body with a trembling hunger he could barely restrain.

Ella gasped as she felt Hassan's intimate possession, momentarily dazed as his enormous length and power began to fill her. Surely he was too big for any woman? For a moment she tensed as she allowed her body to accommodate his and she could feel herself stretching and then settling, her blood pumping and her heart giving a little leap of joy. She made an instinctive sound of pleasure and he looked down at her, smoothing some of her tousled hair from her hot cheeks.

'Does that feel good?' he demanded.

'It feels f-fantastic,' she managed.

'Then let's see if I can make it even better, shall we?'

It sounded like an arrogant sexual boast, but somehow she didn't care. Especially as his words were true. He was making it *irresistible.* And somehow instinct made her respond to him in a way which relegated her relative inexperience to distant memory. Suddenly, she felt like the woman she had thought she could never be. Who could respond with passion and eagerness. No longer a miserable block of ice but a fiery equal who knew exactly what she wanted.

Her hips rose to meet his as she quickly became attuned to each powerful thrust. Clinging to his sweat-sheened back, she felt the powerful play of muscles moving beneath his silken skin as he thrust into her.

'Hassan!' she gasped.

'Ladheedh!' he ground out gutturally, in his native tongue

Helplessly, her head fell back as he kissed her neck and then her breasts, brushing his hungry lips against the tight buds of her nipples, increasing the urgent pleasure which was building inside her with every second.

Hassan groaned. She felt so *hot.* So *tight.* How many nights in the desert had he fantasised about being inside a woman's body like this, before spilling his warm, wet seed onto his own frustrated fingers?

He drove deep inside her before lifting her legs to wrap them around his back so that he could go deeper still. He could feel her fingers digging into his back, could hear her breathless little moans of pleasure as his own began to snowball. Was it because it had been so long that it felt this good? Or because it was so sudden and unexpected, and with none of the usual prerequisites demanded by even the most predatory of women? He felt as if he was clinging by his fingernails to the edge of a cliff, and at any minute he might simply lose control and slip away.

For a moment, he watched her. She looked lost in her own little world: her hair was splayed against the white of the pillow and her lips were parted so that he could see the gleam of her teeth. He watched as her lashes fluttered open so that their gazes locked but he quickly shut his eyes. For why would a man ever choose to let a woman look at him when he was at his most vulnerable?

Instead he began to concentrate on giving her pleasure, and thus taking back the control he had felt in danger of losing. Over and over again, he edged her to the very brink, like a man determined to showcase his repertoire of sensual skills. He heard her murmured little pleas, the entreaties she made, all warm and muffled against his ears.

'What?' he whispered. 'What is it, my fiery little beauty?'

'Please…' Her word trailed away as another wave of sensation swept over her.

He smiled, enjoying his habitual feel of dominance once more. She wasn't so defiant now, was she? 'I can't hear you,' he whispered.

Ella knew what he was doing. He was manipulating her. Playing with her as a cat would a mouse just before it moved in for the kill. She knew how she *should* respond—she should tell him to go to hell—but she was too desperate to hold back. Too eager to experience something which had always remained elusively just out of reach. 'Please, Hassan,' she whimpered. 'Oh, *please.*'

That breathless little plea was his undoing and with one final, powerful thrust he gave her the orgasm she had been begging for, as he had been determined she would do right from the start. But even Hassan could not fail to be carried along on the powerful tide as the spasms began to rack her body and he felt her contracting around him. And somehow, there was a quality in her shuddered little cry which he had never heard before. Something inexplicable which reached out and touched the very heart of him.

Unexpectedly, his own orgasm took him under. It hit him with a powerful force which was strangely bittersweet, so that afterwards he felt as empty as if she had drained him of all life. He heard the shudder of his breath as he sucked air deep into his lungs and felt the sheen of sweat drying on his body. For a few seconds, he felt as close to death as he had ever done in battle, while beneath him, he felt her warm body stir. Long seconds passed before she spoke. He'd been praying that she wouldn't, that instead she would just drift off into sleep and let some of this curious intensity he felt just ebb away. But it was not to be.

'Hassan?' she said drowsily.

'What?'

She swallowed. 'That was...*amazing.*'

'I know it was.'

'I can't believe it happened. It's never—'

'Shh,' he said, because her breathless words were

making him uncomfortable. Carefully, he pulled himself away from her body, his skin beginning to chill as reality slowly returned and he realised what he had done. What a hypocrite he had been! So full of proud words and certainties about the correct and proper way to behave. And yet how could he possibly pass judgement on his friend Alex, when he had proved to be just as weak as he? Despite all his contemptuous words on the subject of suitability, he had taken one of the Jackson sisters to his bed, had stripped her bare and made love to her.

Why the hell had he done *that*?

A cold self-contempt clenched at his heart as he lay there, wondering what he was going to say to her—what *could* he say to her, other than words of bitter regret? But when he turned his head, he saw that she'd fallen asleep, her head pillowed on her arm. She stirred and murmured something, the dark feathered arcs of her lashes fluttering a little. And he held his breath, unaccountably relieved when she turned over and snuggled down against the pillow.

He closed his eyes as he remembered their steamy moves on the dance floor, and then that very public row. She'd left, he'd followed and neither of them had returned. His jaw tightened. What on earth must the other party guests have thought of such behaviour?

And what the hell did he do now?

He *escaped*, that's what he did. Just as if he had been captured by the enemy in battle. He must get away from there before his weak body succumbed and made love to her all over again. Because while once might be regarded as regrettable, twice would be considered a serious error of judgement.

As if on cue, she gave a little moan and snuggled her face deeper into the pillow and, with the skill of the born hunter, he slid noiselessly from the bed. Silently, he collected his discarded clothes, but not before he noticed the silver beads from her ripped dress which lay scattered on the marble floor. With a shudder he imagined the reaction of the palace maids when they arrived to clean his room in the morning. But what was the alternative? That he should start crawling around on his hands and knees, trying to pick them up himself?

In the seclusion of the bathroom, he rapidly pulled on his clothes and from there he made a call to his aide.

Benedict picked up on the second ring. 'Highness?'

Hassan's voice was low. 'Prepare the plane for a flight back to Kashamak. I want to leave as soon as possible.'

'But, Highness, you're supposed to be attending the lunch tomorrow.'

'Well, I won't be,' said Hassan flatly. 'I'll email Alex when I get back. Oh, and Benedict, one more thing.'

'Highness?'

'Have someone bring some women's clothes to my suite first thing in the morning, will you? And before you make any wisecracks, no, I haven't suddenly acquired an appetite for cross-dressing.'

Benedict didn't miss a beat. 'Anything in particular you require, Highness?'

'Something which would be suitable for the lady in question to wear back to her hotel,' said Hassan, pausing as an inconveniently erotic stab of memory made him recall the naked body currently sprawled out on his rumpled sheets. 'American dress size six, I'd imagine.'

CHAPTER FOUR

ELLA stirred, lost in that disorientating split second between sleeping and waking. Where was she? Luxuriously, she stretched her arms above her head. Certainly not at her house in Tooting, that was for sure, because the thunder of lorries past the window was noticeably absent.

The trill of birdsong alerted her at exactly the same time as she registered the soft, moist ache between her legs. And the warm sunlight which bathed her skin. Giving a dreamy little murmur of contentment, she glanced down to see that she was completely naked, and that there were tiny blue marks blooming on her breasts, as if someone had been grazing at them with their teeth. And that was when her memory came rushing back.

Someone *had* been grazing them with their teeth! And a lot more besides.

Sheikh Hassan Al Abbas, to be precise.

With a sharp intake of breath, she grabbed the sheet and pulled it up to her chin. Lying perfectly still, she listened for the sound of movement. Her eyes stole to the other side of the enormous bed, to the rumpled indentation, where Hassan had lain.

So she hadn't imagined it.

Heat flared over her bare skin as vivid images clicked their way into her mind. The way she'd writhed beneath him and *begged* him to make love to her. The way she'd shuddered out his name as he'd made her climax.

She flushed with remembered pleasure. The first and only man ever to have brought her to orgasm and it had to have been *him*.

Her heart pounded. So where the hell was he now?

The bathroom, most probably. She raked her fingers through her tousled hair as she prepared herself for an embarrassing encounter with the man with whom she'd had wild sex the night before.

How *could* she? How could she have fallen into bed with a man who'd made no secret of his contempt for her and her family? Why, he'd barely had to try before she'd allowed him to practically rip her clothes off. Her eyes travelled to the silver dress which lay in a sad little heap on the floor, looking like last year's Christmas decoration, the tiny beads scattered in all directions.

And yet, hadn't he been the most fantastic and unselfish lover, hadn't he destroyed all her doubts and uncertainties along the way? Beneath his expert caresses and amazing lovemaking, he'd made her feel things she'd never felt before. Desire and hunger and *fulfilment*. Like a real woman instead of the frozen and uptight version she'd believed herself to be.

She glanced at the watch which was still on her wrist, appalled to see that it was gone nine. How ironic that the longest sleep she'd had in years should be on the morning when she wasn't even supposed to *be* in the royal palace. She was supposed to be tucked up in that fancy hotel with the rest of her family. What on earth would they say when she didn't turn up for a post-mortem of the party over their breakfast eggs?

Where *was* he?

But even as the true extent of the situation in which she now found herself sank in, Ella made a decision. It had happened and there was absolutely nothing she could do about it. It had been amazing and unexpected and she wasn't going to act all shame-faced and cowed. They had *both* been responsible for what had taken place last night.

And if he decided that he had enjoyed it so much that he wanted to do it all over again, what then? Ella stared at the ceiling, unable to prevent the rush of memories from flooding back. Wouldn't she be only too happy to start over, so they could prove to each other that first impressions needn't necessarily count?

'Hassan?' she called softly.

No answer.

She wondered if he was in the shower, perhaps lathering creamy soap over that honed, olive skin. Suddenly, she could imagine only too well what that might look like. The hard, flat planes of his body. The powerful legs, the taut stomach and the dark mass of hair which grew around his manhood. She closed her eyes. She wasn't going to take herself there. It had been...well, it had been absolutely fantastic. But she wasn't going to read too much into it, not at this stage. All she wanted was to get back to her family as soon as possible, and she needed his help to do that.

'Hassan!' Her voice was louder now but there was still no reply, when just at that moment came a rap at the door.

What should she do?

Ignore it? Wait for Hassan to come out of the bathroom and deal with it himself? Surely, the fewer people who saw her here, the better.

But the rap was repeated and there came the distinct and undeniable sound of someone saying *her* name.

'Miss Jackson?'

Ella screwed up her nose in confusion. That was her. No way on earth she could deny it. How the hell did they know she was here? Wrapping the sheet around her like a fancy-dress version of a Grecian goddess, she padded barefoot to the door, pulling it open and gazing suspiciously through the small crack. Outside stood a tall man she didn't recognise, with a polite smile on his face and what looked like some dry-cleaning hanging over his arm.

'Miss Jackson?' he said again.

Ella screwed her eyes up. 'Who are you?'

'You don't know me. My name is Benedict Austin and I work as an aide to Sheikh Hassan Al Abbas. He asked me to make sure that you got this.'

With this, he handed her the package and Ella blinked. 'What is it?'

'You'll find some clothes in there. The sheikh was most insistent that you have them, since I understand that you…' He hesitated. 'Spilt some wine down your dress last night.'

Ella could feel herself blushing since she suspected that this man knew very well what had *really* happened to her dress. And in that moment, she felt furious. Why couldn't Hassan have had the decency to hand over the clothes himself instead of sending one of his puppets to do the deed? She looked the aide straight in the eye. 'Do you have any idea where he is?'

'The sheikh?' The aide gave an apologetic shrug as if this was a question he had been asked by indignant women many times during his career. 'I'm afraid he had to fly back to Kashamak with some urgency. There were pressing affairs of state which he needed to attend to.'

Ella had thought it wasn't possible to feel any worse than she already did, but this new piece of information just went to show how wrong she could be. So he had done a runner. He had left without even bothering to say goodbye.

Humiliated, she wanted to tell this Benedict Austin just what he could do with his clothes, but pride told her that was a luxury she couldn't afford. What had happened was bad enough, but if she was seen slinking out of the palace wearing a tattered version of last night's dress then she might as well carry a banner, announcing to the world how she'd spent the night.

'Thank you,' she said with as much dignity as she could muster, before taking the proffered package and quietly closing the door on him.

Some women might have cried, but not Ella. She was a survivor. She wasn't about to waste her tears on someone as unworthy as Hassan Al Abbas. Instead she concentrated on making herself presentable enough to find her way out of the strange palace.

A shower and vigorous hair wash got rid of every

last trace of the sheikh's scent from her body, even if the memory of him wasn't quite so easy to shift.

She stared at herself in the mirror, reading the bewilderment which had darkened her blue eyes and wondering why she had behaved like that.

Hadn't she spent her whole life despairing at how easily her mother had capitulated to the whims of her straying ex-husband, allowing him back in her life whenever it pleased him? Time and time again she had begged her mum to grow a little backbone and stand up to the man who'd made such a fool of her. But once she'd realised that her mother would listen to nothing except the demands of her own heart, Ella had vowed that she would be different. *She* would always be coolheaded when it came to men. She would regard them with the same impartiality as she would a prospective business deal.

Up until now, she'd never had a problem with that strategy, but then, up until now she'd never met a man like Hassan Al Abbas. Nor ever felt as if she were a slave to her body. The only sexual experience she'd had prior to last night had been an unmitigated disaster, mainly consisting of her lying looking wide-eyed up at the ceiling, wondering what all the fuss was about.

Well, last night she'd found that out for herself. And suddenly she understood. Suddenly she could see why people took such huge risks when it came to sex. Why they made complete fools of themselves. She felt as if she had been initiated to a secret club, without having decided whether or not she really wanted to be a member.

With trembling fingers, she opened up the package which Hassan's aide had brought with him. Inside lay a cool white dress and a pair of panties nestling among sheets of tissue paper. But while the dress was a fairly respectable length, the panties were nothing but a peach-coloured thong, a sexy little garment which revealed more than it concealed. The thin, satin string made her bottom look almost bare and the filmy peach fabric at the front showed the dark fuzz of hair through which Hassan had hungrily tangled his fingers only hours before.

Her skin felt tainted as she put it on, yet what choice did she have but to wear it? Had *he* chosen it, she wondered, or did he usually leave that kind of thing to his aide?

Slapping on some makeup from her purse and a defiant slash of scarlet lipstick, she stuffed her ruined silver dress into the bathroom bin, sickeningly aware that there were tiny beads lying all over the floor. And then, having forced her feet into what was quite clearly a pair of evening shoes, she let herself out of the suite, momentarily trying to get her bearings.

Heading towards a wide corridor hung with lavish chandeliers she caught a glimpse of perfectly manicured grass in the distance and realised that she must be near the palace gardens. Could she find some passing member of staff and ask them to arrange a car to take her back to the hotel? Was that possible?

'Miss Jackson? Miss Jackson, isn't it?'

The icily cultured voice behind her made Ella freeze in horror because she couldn't fail to recognise those aristocratic tones. Oh, please don't let it be Queen Zoe, she prayed silently, her hopes crumbling as she turned round to stare into the cold features of her sister's future mother-in-law.

Awkwardly, Ella bobbed a curtsey, her cheeks burning with embarrassment. 'Er, good morning, Your Majesty.'

'It's Ella, isn't it?'

'That's right, Your Majesty.'

The queen raised her eyebrows. 'Forgive me for being a little surprised to see you here at such an hour. I thought that you and your family were staying at the hotel?'

Ella hoped her grimace resembled a smile. What could she do, other than be evasive? Tell the queen that she'd spent the night with the sheikh? Wasn't the fact that she was creeping around the corridors wearing new clothes which didn't match last night's shoes evidence enough? 'I…I fell asleep,' she said lamely.

There was a silence while Ella dared the queen to ask just *where* she'd fallen asleep. But fortunately, good breeding must have stopped her, for the older woman simply gave a disapproving look, as if she didn't believe a word of it.

'I see. And have you had breakfast?' asked the queen.

'Er, no. I'm not really very hungry, Your Majesty. In fact, I really ought to be getting back to the hotel. My mother will be wondering where I am.'

'Yes, I can imagine she will be,' answered the queen drily. 'Well, speak to one of the staff and they will arrange a car for you.'

'Thank you, Your Majesty.' Ella gave the deepest

curtsey she could manage and waited until the queen gave a brief nod before walking off.

It took her a while, but eventually she found someone and made herself understood well enough to order a car.

Minutes later she was being driven along a picturesque coastal road, grateful to put miles between herself and the Santina royal palace. But Ella's stomach was in knots and she barely noticed the deep sapphire of the sea or the perfect blue of the sky. For once, the island's scenic beauty left her cold.

All she could think about was the way she'd behaved. It was not only completely uncharacteristic, it was also shameful, because she had chosen the worst man in the world with whom to be sexually rampant. She'd been given the perfect opportunity to prove to Hassan Al Abbas that his bias against the Jackson family was unfair and unfounded. Yet instead, she had simply reinforced all those prejudices with her own behaviour. He'd accused the women in her family of behaving like cheap tramps and hadn't she gone ahead and done just that?

Ella bit her lip as the car began to snake down the road towards the hotel. She'd let everyone down. But most of all, she'd let herself down.

And she was the one who had to live with what she'd done.

CHAPTER FIVE

'I DON'T care how you do it. Just do it!' The woman's voice was shrill and insistent. 'It's my wedding day and I've dreamt about it for too long to make any kind of compromise.'

'I'll work something out,' promised Ella, replacing the phone with a heavy sigh, which wasn't entirely due to the latest unreasonable request from one of her high-profile clients. Since the earliest days of her thriving events company, Cinderella-Rockerfella, she'd been asked for many bizarre things, and usually she took them all in her stride. But usually she wasn't feeling a mixture of guilt and general queasiness, the way she'd been feeling nonstop since she'd returned from her sister's royal engagement party.

Nothing she did seemed to help. She found herself wishing she could forget the sheikh who had given her so much pleasure when he'd taken her to his bed. But what she wished even more was that she could rid herself of the nagging fear which was growing by the day. The fear which this morning had manifested itself in bringing up her breakfast only minutes after she'd eaten it.

With an effort, she forced the worrying thoughts

from her head and looked up at Daisy, her assistant, an efficient twenty-two-year-old whose high energy levels had recently made Ella feel as if she was about a hundred.

'What kind of couple wants to sit on matching thrones for their wedding ceremony, Daisy?' she asked wearily.

'A couple with massive egos?' suggested Daisy with a grin. 'But I guess that isn't so surprising. Two music stars that huge are bound to want to make a splash, especially as they've sold the photo rights to *Celebrity!* magazine. And anyway, you couldn't be better placed to organise something like that, could you, Ella, since your own sister is actually marrying a *real-life royal*!'

'Please don't remind me,' said Ella with a wince.

'Why not? Most people would be revelling in the reflected glory, yet you've hardly said a word about the engagement party since you got back and that was weeks ago,' grumbled Daisy. 'I had to read about it for myself in all the papers.'

'Well, there you go.' Ella realised that her fingers were trembling and she put down the black felt-tip pen with which she'd been doodling. She looked down and saw that she had actually drawn a *sword* by the side of her notes. What the hell did *that* mean? 'Daisy, will you try to organise two golden thrones for me? Ring up that theatrical props company we sometimes use and see if they can help out. I…well, I have to go out this afternoon.' She stood too quickly and her head spun like a merry-go-round. It had been doing a lot of that lately.

Daisy glanced at her. 'Ella, are you okay? You've gone a really funny colour.'

'No, I'm fine,' said Ella, swallowing down the increasingly familiar taste of nausea which was rising in her throat. 'I'll see you later.'

Blanking the concerned look of her assistant, she walked out into the busy London street where an unseasonal shower was in full pelt and she realised too late that she wasn't wearing her raincoat. But who cared about getting caught in the rain, or ostentatious last-minute additions to showbiz weddings, when there was something so big in your head it was beginning to dominate everything you did?

She was shivering as she took a bus to her house in Tooting. It wasn't the most fashionable post code in town but it was well served by public transport and had the added bonus of being cheap. Living there meant she didn't have to live in a shoebox and she'd been able to plough any spare cash into her thriving little business. The business she'd worked so hard to get off the ground, because she'd wanted to be an independent woman, determined that she would never have to rely on the whims of a man for her income or livelihood.

And the thought which was echoing round and round in her head was: *What's going to happen to your precious business now, if your worst fears are confirmed?*

The house felt cold when she entered and she went straight into the bathroom where the pregnancy testing kit she'd bought was still sitting unused next to the toothpaste. For a moment she just stared at it before pulling it off the shelf with hands which were shaking, knowing that she couldn't put off the moment of truth any longer.

Her heart was pounding as she tore open the cardboard box and as she crouched over the loo, attempting to pee onto the narrow little stick, she thought how surreal this felt. This is what millions of women all over the world have done, she told herself. Were probably doing even now. But she'd bet all the money in her purse that not one of them was doing it as the result of a one-night stand with an empty-eyed sheikh who'd left her without even bothering to say goodbye.

She didn't need to see the blue line on the stick to know that the test was positive. She'd known that in her heart all along. Forcing herself to make a cup of hot, sweet tea, she took it into the sitting room and sat drinking it as the light began to fade from the sky. One by one, the pinpoints of stars began to speckle the sky and all she could think about was the single fact which was going to change her life for ever.

She was pregnant.

Pregnant by the sheikh.

She was going to have an unplanned baby by a man who despised her and all she stood for. Ella put down her empty teacup and closed her eyes. It didn't really get much worse than that, did it?

Yet it was strange what tricks the mind could play. For a few weeks more, Ella pretended it wasn't happening. She let the secret grow inside her head as well as inside her belly and she was slim enough for it not to notice. It was as if, by not telling anyone else, she could almost convince herself that it wasn't happening. But aligned with this lack of logic was the overwhelming desire to tell *someone*, to unburden herself to someone who might understand.

Not her mother. Definitely not her weak, romantic mother. Not her sisters either—not if she didn't want word to get out. And definitely not her father. Ella shuddered. Her father would go *mental* if he found out.

Which left Ben, her brother. Brilliant Ben, who, for all his reputation as a control-freak tycoon, was fiercely protective when it came to the women in his family. He was currently living in some splendour in a beach house on the island of Santina while he worked on a charity project. Before she had time to change her mind, Ella picked up the phone and dialled his number.

'Ben Jackson.'

'Ben, it's Ella.'

The rather abrupt note in his voice gave way to one of softening affection. 'Ella,' he murmured. 'Who I still haven't quite forgiven for leaving the island in such dramatic fashion after the engagement party. Why the hell didn't you come to the lunch the next day? I was looking forward to a catch-up.'

'Actually, the reason I didn't come to the lunch is sort of the same reason why I'm ringing you now.'

His voice was teasing. 'Am I supposed to guess what that is, or are you going to cut to the chase?'

Ella swallowed, instinctively knowing that this was the kind of news no brother wanted to receive. And that there was no way of saying it which could possibly lessen its impact. 'Ben, I'm pregnant.'

There was a pause.

'But you don't have a boyfriend, Ella—or at least,

you didn't the last time I spoke to you. Which happened to be at the engagement party. What's going on?' His voice roughened in a way she hadn't heard it do for years. 'Who's the father?'

Ella felt stricken with shame, wishing that she'd never made this wretched call, knowing that she was about to fall off her sainted little-sister pedestal, big-time. But telling someone made it real, and that was the sorry truth of it—it *was* real. She couldn't hide from the reality any longer. And it was pointless trying to lie or to make the truth more palatable by putting some kind of gloss on it. Dreading her brother's reaction to her next piece of news, she licked her lips.

'His name is Hassan Al Abbas.'

There was another brief silence, and when he spoke, Ben's voice had taken on an entirely different tone. 'The sheikh?'

'That's the one.'

'You're having the baby of one of the most powerful men in the Middle East?'

Ella shivered. It sounded even more daunting when he put it like that. 'So it would seem.' She heard her brother utter a few terse expletives. 'Ben, don't swear!'

'What do you expect me to do?' he retorted savagely. 'Have you thought about what you're letting yourself in for? Don't you know what a reputation he has? Hell, Ella, I didn't even know you two were an item.'

'We're not!' she put in fiercely. 'We are most emphatically not. We…we met. We fought and then…then…'

'I think I can work out the rest for myself,' he said quickly. 'The question is what you're going to do about it?'

Ella's hand strayed to her stomach. A still-flat stomach, it was true, but not for much longer. Deep inside her was growing a tiny embryo which was half that black-eyed brute of a man, but also half *her*. Half Jackson. Bobby and Julie's first grandchild. A first nephew or niece for her brothers and sisters. A new life about to enter her crazy and dysfunctional family. A terrible pain clutched at her heart as she thought of the heavy burden of responsibility which now hung over her, but knowing, too, that there was only one thing she could do. And fast following on that pain came a powerful wave of protectiveness. A determination that something good would come out of this whole mess.

'I'm going to keep the baby,' she said fiercely.

'Good.' Ben let out a long and ragged sigh. 'That's good. And what about Al Abbas? What does he say about it all?'

'I haven't told him. And he won't want to be the father, Ben.' Her voice was flat as she remembered the way he'd snuck out of her bed, like a thief in the middle of the night. 'He doesn't even like me!'

There was a pause. 'So are you *going* to tell him?'

Again, she thought of Hassan. Not the man who had seduced her with such ease and shown her what true pleasure could be. But the other side of that same man. She remembered the strange, cold emptiness she'd seen in his eyes and a shiver rippled down her spine. 'I don't *know*,' she said desperately.

'You know that it'll be irrevocable once you do,

and that you'll have little control over what happens next?' he warned. 'That not only is he unimaginably wealthy, he is also an autocrat. Men like that are possessive about what is theirs, and he will see this baby as belonging to him. He's *ruthless*, sis—make no mistake about that.'

Ben's words told her nothing she didn't already know and part of her wanted to steer clear of Hassan in order to protect herself and her baby. Ella felt the drumming of her heart as she worked out what she wanted to do. If she could wave a magic wand, it would be to erase all memory of the heartless sheikh from her life. But this wasn't just about *her* any more, was it? There was a child involved and didn't Hassan have the right to know about the existence of that child, no matter what their feelings for each other were?

'I have no choice but to tell him,' she said quietly.

Ben's voice sounded gruff. 'Actually, you *do* have a choice. I just hope he appreciates the one you've made. Let me know if there's anything I can do. And I mean *anything*.'

'I will. Thanks, Ben.' Ella swallowed down the sudden lump which had risen in her throat. 'Oh, and Ben? You won't tell anyone else about this, will you?'

'Not unless you want me to. Let's hold off the hysterical reaction from the rest of the clan for as long as possible, shall we?'

Ella was thoughtful as she replaced the phone, realising that she couldn't put off telling Hassan a moment longer. Until she also realised that she knew very little about him, other than that he was a sheikh. She didn't even know where he lived! She frowned.

Hadn't his aide mentioned a country when he'd delivered her the dress and the insultingly sexy thong? Kasha-something. Kashamak?

She sat down at her computer and tapped the name into the search engine to discover that Kashamak was indeed a country, and that Hassan was its supreme ruler, although he had a younger brother.

She stared at a photo of him, clad in what was clearly his national dress, and thought how formidable he looked. His thick black hair was covered by a white headdress, held in place by a dark, knotted silk cord. It made him look more *foreign.* More unapproachable.

It was strange to stare at the sensual curve of his mouth and to remember how thoroughly it had explored her body. She remembered the powerful orgasm which had shaken her to the core, the first one she'd ever experienced. Was that what had made the sex seem so profound to her, or was that just the effect he had on all women?

With an effort, she dragged her eyes away from the photo. There were whole pages of facts about Kashamak's huge natural resources and the border disputes with one of the neighbouring countries, which Hassan had recently settled, but Ella barely took anything else in. She didn't *need* to know that to his country he was a hero, because the whole point of looking at all this stuff had a purpose. She now knew where he was based, but how did you go about contacting a man who was so obviously out of reach? His very position isolated him from people like her and he certainly hadn't left behind his mobile number and told her to be in touch, had he?

In the end, she summoned up the courage to ask her sister Allegra, who in turn asked Alex, who said, regretfully, that he couldn't really hand Hassan's number out to anyone, not even family. Security issues, he explained. But he would pass on her details to the sheikh and ask him to be in touch with her.

Ella felt mortified when this piece of information was relayed to her, though she supposed she should be grateful that her sister hadn't demanded to know *why* she wanted to contact Hassan. She guessed she was so bound up in her own impending marriage that she hadn't quizzed her about their smoochy dancing. Or mentioned the subsequent stand-up row on the dance floor....

A sense of frustration caught hold of her and she wondered what Hassan might think when he heard about her efforts to contact him. What if he failed to get in touch? What if he thought she was just a woman on the make who couldn't accept that he hadn't wanted to see her again?

At this, Ella brightened a little. That might be the best of all possible worlds. She would have appeased her conscience by trying to contact him, but there would then be no need to involve him in her baby's life.

Galvanised into action, she made an appointment with her doctor and went to see him the very next morning. Somehow it made her feel better to have done something really positive. Having her blood pressure taken and being checked out and told that she was perfectly healthy filled her with a feeling of hope for the future. She could do this. She *would* do this.

Lots of women brought up babies on their own, and some of them even ran their own businesses!

Later, she collected a cappuccino and an apple doughnut from the coffee shop near the headquarters of Cinderella-Rockerfella and realised that it was the first time she'd felt properly hungry in days. Swinging the brown paper bag from her fingers, she walked into the office and greeted Daisy with a smile, wondering why her assistant's face looked so peculiar.

'Are you all right, Daisy?'

Rather dramatically, Daisy started jerking her head in the direction of Ella's office. 'In *there*,' she said in a stage whisper.

'In where, what?' asked Ella, confused. But her confusion quickly morphed into something else, something she could never have put a name to but which felt like terror and excitement and a sudden cold dread all swirled together as she reached for the door handle.

Drawing a deep breath, she walked into her tiny office, shocked but somehow not surprised to see the towering form of Sheikh Hassan Al Abbas silhouetted against the window.

CHAPTER SIX

ELLA's heart missed a beat as the sheikh's powerful body managed to block out most of the available light. And not just the light. It was as if he had sucked all the oxygen out of the atmosphere, making it suddenly very difficult for her to breathe. 'Wh-what are you doing here?' she whispered.

Hassan stared at the woman who had just walked into the cluttered office. The only colour in her pale face was the scarlet lipstick which coloured her unsmiling lips and he found himself thinking that she looked like a stranger. But she *was* a stranger, he reminded himself grimly, one he'd only ever seen beneath the false glittering light of chandeliers. Or naked, of course.

'You wanted to see me, Ella,' he said softly. 'So here I am.'

The shock of seeing him again felt like a physical blow and Ella put her doughnut and coffee down on the desk, afraid that her trembling fingers would spill the scalding liquid. 'I wanted to *speak* to you. There's a difference.' She met his black, empty eyes, furious with her body for the instinctive little tremble it gave. As if it was recognising that here was a man who had the power to turn her into a trembling mass of longing. Who could breathe danger into her heart. With an effort, she dragged her attention back to his sombre face. 'Do you always turn up in someone's office unannounced? It's certainly an unconventional approach.'

'Ah, but I'm an unconventional man in many ways. In others, of course, I can be rather more predictable.' His black eyes flicked over her, thinking how tired she looked. 'And since we didn't make any arrangement to hook up again, I'm curious to know what it is you want?'

Ella was finding it hard to cling onto her equilibrium. His appearance here had taken her by surprise, but that wasn't the only reason for the sudden racing of her heart. It was *him.* The effect he was having on her, no matter how hard she tried to remain immune to him. And seeing him in the flesh again was infinitely more powerful than studying a photograph on the Net.

The night they'd…met, he had been wearing a formal tuxedo, which flattered even the plainest-looking man. And this was a man who certainly had no need of flattery. Today he wore an expensive suit, the kind worn by successful businessmen the world over. And yet he did not seem to wear it comfortably. It seemed too constricting for the powerful lines of his body. Already, he had undone a button of his shirt and must have tugged impatiently at his tie. Ella suddenly became aware that beneath all the royal trappings lurked a very primitive man, and the enormity of what she was about to tell him filled her with dread.

But first it was important to establish some kind of

dialogue. There were a couple of things she needed to clear up, no matter what happened afterwards, because surely the answers to her questions would determine just how he viewed women in general, and her in particular.

'So tell me, Hassan,' she said in a low voice. 'Do you always leave a woman's bed in the middle of the night, without even bothering to say goodbye to her?'

He was surprised by her directness and more than a little irritated by her lack of remorse. Didn't she feel even a shred of shame over what had happened? he wondered. Or were one-night stands a regular occurrence in her life? His jaw tightened, unwilling to accept that he had chosen a woman who spread her favours freely, and yet, given her background, why was he so surprised?

'I decided that leaving when I did was the best form of damage limitation,' he said flatly.

'Excuse me? Did you say *damage* limitation?'

'Oh, come on. Let's not dress it up to be something it wasn't,' he said, shrugging off her outrage. 'It was great sex—we both know that—but under the circumstances, it was ill-advised. It wasn't going anywhere. It never could. So what would have been the point in prolonging it?'

'Surely good manners might have prompted you to say some sort of goodbye?'

He gave a short laugh. 'I think we abandoned good manners some time after you threw champagne in my face.'

'And they were certainly a distant memory by the time you ripped my dress off.'

Hassan's mouth hardened, because her defiant words were exciting him. And this was exactly what he hadn't wanted: to be reminded of just how completely he had fallen victim to her vixen charms. He remembered the soft yield of her bare breasts beneath his calloused fingers and felt a savage jerk of lust, along with a stab of self-contempt. For what use was a man who could defeat his enemies in battle if he then allowed himself to weaken in the arms of a woman he despised?

'You got the replacement dress and underwear I sent?'

'Yes, I got them,' she snapped. 'I happened to be wearing them when I bumped into Queen Zoe in the palace corridors on my way out.'

He winced. 'What did she say?'

'Oh, she's too polite to say anything much, although her face was a picture. Especially when I told her that I'd spent the night with you.'

Hassan looked at her in horror. 'You *told* her you spent the night with me?'

Briefly, Ella allowed herself to enjoy his discomfiture until she reminded herself that this was not about scoring points. 'No, of course I didn't tell her. But I wish I had. The high and mighty sheikh who'd made no secret of his contempt for the Jacksons, actually ending up in bed with one of them! That would have provided plenty of fuel for the gossips, wouldn't it?'

For a moment, Hassan almost smiled, because nobody could deny that she had spirit as well as beauty, and no woman had ever spoken to him in such a way before. If she was not who she was then he might have enjoyed a short and mutually satisfying affair with her, laying down his usual ground rules of no commitment before it commenced.

But that was not going to happen.

Not with Ella Jackson.

He looked around her office, his mouth flattening with distaste as he took in its garish appearance. It was as tacky as he'd imagined when the investigator he'd hired had told him that she ran an events company called Cinderella-Rockerfella.

The walls were covered with glossy photos of events she had presumably organised—ghastly montages of occasions which looked like the height of vulgarity. There was an enormous blown-up wedding photo of a couple he vaguely recognised, an international footballer and his bride. That the woman was wearing a gown which seemed to reveal most of her surgically enhanced breasts seemed to Hassan to mock at the very sanctity of marriage and respect for her groom. Why, she might as well have taken her vows naked, he thought in disgust, wondering how Ella could bear to work for such people.

Because she's a Jackson, that's why. She *is* one of these people.

'So why were you trying to contact me?' he questioned softly.

His question brought reality crashing back into her thoughts and Ella's heart began to pound. 'No ideas?'

'Plenty.' He looked into her eyes and remembered thrusting into her so deep that it felt as if he was in danger of losing himself in the process.

'Oh?'

'Maybe you decided your night with me was so hot that you wanted a repeat of it. I wouldn't blame you if you did.'

Ella was appalled at her answering stab of desire and even more appalled by his out-and-out arrogance. 'I try never to make the same mistake twice, Hassan. Any other suggestions?'

Dark clouds drifted into his mind. He made himself say it as a safeguard. In the same way that people often forced themselves to confront a worst-case scenario, thinking that if they did, it meant it would never come true.

'Or our ill-judged liaison has left us with something other than regrets.'

She stared at him, because didn't his words make what she was about to tell him even more difficult? 'That's the most cold-hearted description I've ever heard,' she whispered.

Her lack of denial unsettled him but Hassan kept his nerve, the same way he'd kept it when someone had once held the blade of a knife to his throat. In that moment, he had thought he was going to die. But he hadn't died, had he? He had defied the odds and lived to fight another day. 'That's because I am a cold-hearted man, Ella. Be in no doubt of that. And I haven't come here to play guessing games. What is it that you want to say to me?'

'That you're right!' She swallowed as she forced out the bitter truth. 'That we have been left with something—or rather, I have.' She looked into the narrowed black eyes and spoke in a low voice. 'I'm having a baby, Hassan.'

Hassan swallowed, remembering the way that the knife blade had nicked against his skin, a wound made to warn him rather than to slay him. But the flesh had healed, hadn't it? While this…*this*…

This would not heal!

He took a step towards her, his voice low and urgent, his eyes locking on hers as if looking for the essential flaw in her argument. 'But not necessarily my baby?'

'Of course it's your baby!'

'There's no *of course* about it,' he denied as the rush of blood to his head threatened to deafen him. 'You fell into my bed with a speed which is unequalled—even in my experience. How am I to know that you don't do that with a different man every night of the week?'

His words hurt, as no doubt he intended them to, but Ella didn't show it. She forced herself to be logical rather than emotional, the way she'd had to be for most of her life. Because could she really blame him for jumping to such a conclusion, when all he had was the evidence of how she'd behaved?

She realised that he was lashing out at her because of what she'd just told him. That he was scared. Because what man would jump for joy at being informed that a total stranger was having their baby? He probably thought she was trying to railroad him into marriage or commitment—he was certainly arrogant enough for that. Well, maybe it was time to reassure him that she could manage perfectly well on her own.

'Because actually, I don't sleep around, though of course you're perfectly at liberty not to believe me,' she said quietly.

'You made an exception just for me, did you?'

'There's no need for false modesty, Hassan. I'm sure plenty of women have made an exception for you in the past.' But stupidly, that hurt too. Why on earth should it hurt to think of him in bed with other women? She sucked in a deep breath. 'I realise this has come as a shock to you—'

'Oh, the mistress of all understatement!' he mocked, because somehow mockery was easier than having to acknowledge that what she said was true. And that even as she stood there in her blue silk dress, with her scarlet lips trembling, his child was growing deep inside her.

'But I want you to know that I am planning to have this baby and to keep it and to…to love it.' She saw his mouth twist with derision and she guessed what he thought was about to follow. 'And I'm not asking you for anything.'

He gave a cynical laugh. 'That really would be a first. So why bother telling me?'

'Because you're the father and I felt it was my duty to let you know.'

Hassan stilled as he plucked one word from her breathless sentence.

Duty.

It was a word which had made him the man he was. A word his own mother had rejected, causing irreparable damage to their royal house and wrecking three lives in the process. Wasn't it now his duty to stand by and support this woman, no matter how much he abhorred the idea?

'This is like some bad dream,' he said suddenly.

Ella nodded. Because hadn't she thought exactly the same? 'It came as a shock to me too,' she admitted.

He shook his head. 'But I made sure that I was careful.'

'I know you did.'

He wondered how it could have happened and then remembered the way his hands had trembled as he had pulled on the protection.... 'Just not careful enough,' he said bitterly as he looked into her ice-blue eyes. 'Call it weakness—yes, why *don't* we call it weakness?—but having you writhing all over my bed made my attention to detail a little lacking! I'd been away fighting a war and it was a long time since I'd been with a woman. What's your excuse?'

'My *excuse* is that I had a momentary lapse of judgement,' she said, not wanting to tell him that he had blown her away. Because wouldn't that make him even more arrogant and unreasonable? 'As it happens, I'm pretty much a novice when it comes to sex—'

'You weren't acting much like a novice that night.'

'Maybe that has more to do with your breadth of experience rather than my lack of it,' she answered. 'There's no point in us arguing about it. I just felt you had a right to know that you'd fathered a child. And now you do. I've discharged my duty. So if you wouldn't mind leaving, I really do have work to get on with.'

He read defiance in her eyes. It was not an emotion he encountered very often and, to his surprise, he realised that she meant it. That she was not posturing or making empty threats in order to impress him—that she *actually wanted him to leave*!

The contrary side of his nature made him want to rebel against a woman trying to dictate what his behaviour should be. But so did something else. He felt the sudden twisting of his gut as a rush of unwanted emotion hit him. For a moment, the pain of it took him back to a time he had buried deeper than the most precious artifacts which surrounded his father's tomb. The time when his mother had walked away to be with the man she 'loved.' Leaving behind a small and confused little boy who had vowed fiercely never to allow himself to be hurt as his father had been…

And then the dark mist of memory cleared and he found himself staring into the ice-blue eyes of Ella Jackson.

She was having his baby, he realised incredulously. And therefore this was not just any baby. The child she carried was the son or daughter of the sheikh. And it was *his*. *His*.

He had once vowed never to marry. He had told his younger brother that one day the sheikhdom would be his—for no child would ever spring from the loins of Hassan Al Abbas. Blighted by the pain he had felt at his mother's desertion, he had known that fatherhood would never be on his agenda, but now suddenly it was.

His mouth hardened and the hands which had hung by the sides of his powerful thighs now clenched into fists, because he recognised in that instant that what Ella Jackson had told him had changed his life irrevocably. In that moment, all his plans and certainties underwent a dramatic transformation and he knew what he must do. More importantly, what he must *not* do. He would not do as his own mother had done. He would not turn his back on his own flesh and blood.

He leaned towards her. 'I'm not going anywhere. We need to talk,' he said grimly.

She eyed him warily, his disturbing proximity reminding her that he was dangerous in more ways than one. 'I thought we'd said everything there was to say.'

'Are you kidding? We haven't even touched the surface, Ella. Or did you think you could get away with telling me that you're having my child and I would just walk away and leave you to get on with it?'

Yes, maybe she had. Maybe she had been that stupid and naive. Maybe she'd hoped that fate, or his reluctance to acknowledge his baby, would have taken him out of her life for good. But not any more. There was no mistaking the dark determination which had made his face look even more intimidating and something about his stance made her realise there was trouble ahead. The phone on her desk began to ring and automatically Ella reached out her hand to answer it.

'Leave it,' he bit out.

'I can't leave it. It's my—'

'I said, *leave* it. Let the other girl answer it.'

Their eyes met in silent combat as the phone rang six times before Daisy picked it up in the outer office and Ella knew this was a fight she would not win. Because how could she possibly conduct a business conversation with one of her clients under the grim gaze of the sheikh? She wouldn't trust him not to snatch the phone right out of her hand and slam it down. And what if Daisy heard them arguing through the thin walls? 'Okay, I'll talk to you,' she conceded wearily. 'But not now and not here. I'll meet you later, when I've finished work.'

'Good.' He held her gaze for a moment. 'Come and have dinner in my hotel suite.'

She shook her head. 'There's no way I'm coming to your hotel.'

'No?' He saw the parting of her luscious scarlet lips and felt an unwilling kick of lust. But wouldn't bedding her only be counterproductive to the idea which was slowly forming in his mind? An idea he would need to broach very carefully in order to get her to accept it...

'Then where else do you suggest?' he continued. 'If we have what will inevitably be a difficult conversation in a crowded restaurant, we risk being overheard by waiters or other diners. And I don't want to find our meeting making headlines in tomorrow's newspapers.'

Ella heard the undeniable command in his voice and part of her wanted to rebel against it. He was so unashamedly autocratic, she thought. So completely used to getting his own way. If she went to his hotel suite then wouldn't that allow him to call the shots? She didn't know what he was going to say but she knew she needed all her wits about her, and maybe the best way of ensuring that was to be on home territory.

'You can come to my house instead,' she said. 'Get the address from Daisy on your way out. I'll see you there at nine, but you'd better have eaten something first. I'm not planning on making you dinner.'

He paused for a moment as he went to pass her, studying the dark spill of her silken hair and the scarlet tremble of her lips. The desire to kiss her was overwhelming. But he fought it as he had fought so much else in his life.

'I'll be there,' he said softly, ignoring the dark dilatation of her eyes as he walked out of the office without another word.

CHAPTER SEVEN

WITH his bodyguards sitting grim-faced in two waiting cars, Hassan rang the doorbell, briefly wondering if he'd got the wrong address. He frowned. This neighbourhood was like no other he'd ever seen and Ella's house was in a row of other small houses which looked directly onto a busy main road.

He didn't know anyone who lived in a place like this—the kind of place you lived in when you didn't have a lot of money to splash around. And yet Ella Jackson had blended in perfectly at the royal engagement party in her sparkling silver dress, her sky-high heels and those gleaming scarlet lips. He'd thought she'd be living somewhere trashy and flashy, displaying the complete lack of taste which had been on show in her office today. Not in this rather ordinary little house which was situated on the wrong side of town.

The door opened and Ella stood there, confounding yet another of his preconceptions. Gone was the silk and the gloss. With her shiny hair tugged into a ponytail, she was wearing a plain white T-shirt and faded blue jeans which emphasised the blueness of her eyes. He frowned. Gone too was that shiny red lipstick which drew attention to the luscious mouth which made a man have sinful thoughts, no matter how hard he tried not to. She was scarcely recognisable from the slick party girl he'd met, and for a moment, he felt disorientated, as if she had suddenly produced some low-key twin sister.

'This is where you live?' he questioned slowly.

'No, I thought I'd rent the place out in order to impress you, but I can see that I've failed.' She pulled the door open and ushered him in, stupidly unprepared for the tingling response of her body as she looked up at him. 'Yes, it's where I live, Hassan. Why, did you think I'd be living in some over-the-top boudoir, all gilt and ceiling mirrors and shaggy fur rugs lying all over the place?'

Actually, this was so close to what he *had* been thinking that for a moment he didn't answer. Instead he stepped into the small hallway, shutting the door behind him. From there he followed the blue-jeaned sway of her bottom into what should have been the sitting room.

Except that this wasn't what it seemed either. The surprisingly large space contained a sofa and a couple of chairs, but these were all bunched up at one end, as if they were nothing but an afterthought. Pride of place had been given instead to an easel, on which stood a half-finished painting of a naked man. It looked pretty good from where Hassan stood but his critical judgment was suspended as he made the inevitable comparison. He emerged from that with his ego satisfied but his morals outraged by the thought that she must have spent time studying another man's genitals.

'Who is this?' he demanded furiously.

'That's none of your business.'

'On the contrary.' His eyes glittered. 'You carry the child of the sheikh and that *makes* it my business! Who is he?'

Ella heard the control-freak quality in his voice and it set off more warning bells in her head. She'd been wondering how this meeting was going to proceed and now she had her first indication. Was he going to play high-handed and possessive with all that 'child of the sheikh' stuff? Her first instinct was to tell him to go to hell but some deep-rooted protectiveness told her not to inflame him. That he was not a man to make an enemy of, especially in these circumstances.

'He's an architectural student who poses in my life-drawing class.'

'You have had sex with him?'

'Of course I haven't had sex with him! I hardly know—' Too late she stopped herself as she realised the irony of her words, but not before a look of bitter triumph had filled his empty eyes with a dark light.

'You hardly know him?' he finished acidly. 'You hardly knew me either, but that didn't stop you opening up your milky-pale thighs for me, did it, Ella?'

Ella bit back the angry retort which hovered on her lips, telling herself that it didn't matter. He was here to talk about the baby and that was the only thing which mattered.

'We could waste a lot of time insulting each other, but I'm too tired to want to. And that's not why you're here, is it?' She flashed him a polite smile. 'So in the spirit of trying to conduct this conversation in a civilised way, perhaps you'd like to sit down?'

'No, I'll stand, thanks.' For the first time in a long while, he realised that he had no game plan to follow, and no idea of how to get what he wanted from this woman. Although ironically, he still wasn't quite sure *what* he wanted.

Restlessly, he went to look out of the window, just as a large red bus lumbered to a halt and discharged a group of teenagers who stood in noisy conversation right outside. When he turned back to face her, his expression was as perplexed as the grim faces of his waiting bodyguards. 'Why do you live in a place like this, Ella?'

'Why do you think? Because I like the sound of the traffic?' She met his grim expression and shrugged. 'It's what I can afford, Hassan, that's why. Any available money I have goes straight back into the business, rather than being wasted on paying a high rent.'

'Your father doesn't give you an allowance?'

Ella almost laughed out loud, wondering what kind of planet he was on. Or maybe it was a mark of her father's chameleon-like qualities that he could still manage to convince the world that there was money in the family.

'No. I don't get anything from my father.'

He heard the acid note which had tinged her voice and for the second time that day he noticed the faint blue shadows beneath her eyes. *Didn't pregnant women suffer excessively from fatigue?* A sudden pang of guilt washed over him. 'Perhaps we will sit after all,' he said unexpectedly, putting his hand on the small of her back and guiding her towards one of the chairs. 'You look a little tired.'

Ella didn't have the energy to object, but the small act of kindness left her feeling dangerously vulnerable. And she *was* tired. All the emotions which had accumulated over the past few weeks had left her so wrung out that it was as much as she could do not to put her head in her hands and weep.

She thought about all the plans she'd made for the future. All her strategies for exploiting a gap in the market and making a success of herself. Her determination that she should earn a decent living for herself and never have to rely on a faithless man, the way her mother had done.

Where were all those plans now?

Up in the air, that's where. Because every woman knew that a baby meant a major career juggle, whether you were single or not. And now she had to deal with a powerful and dauntingly sexy man who she suspected was going to try to outwit her. *And she still didn't know what it was he wanted.*

He waited until she was settled before he sat on the sofa opposite her, his long legs stretched out in front of him, his black eyes enigmatic and watchful.

'So when is the baby due?'

'Well, it's been fourteen weeks since the party, which means the baby's due in January.' She looked at him steadily. 'January 8, to be precise.'

Hassan tensed, because having an actual *date* to focus on changed everything. It transformed her pregnancy from a dark and unknown spectre into something real. Something which was happening. To her and to *him.* For a moment there was silence while he tried to make sense of her words. That early in the new year, as the snows were falling onto the highest peaks of the Samaltyn Mountains, he would become a father.

'This is momentous news,' he said slowly.

'Yes.'

'Who else have you told?'

She hesitated. 'Only my brother, Ben.'

'He is discreet?'

She heard the doubt in his voice and bristled. 'Actually, there's nobody as discreet as Ben, though you probably find that difficult to believe as he happens to be a dreaded *Jackson*.'

'Actually, I happen to know that in the business world your brother has a formidable reputation,' conceded Hassan drily. 'But this is something very different.'

The nod to Ben's undoubted talent should have pleased her but Ella was too concerned with the implication behind Hassan's question to do anything but stare at him in growing horror. 'Why are you so concerned who knows about this? You think...you think...' She sucked in a deep and unsteady breath and expelled it again on a horrified shudder. 'Listen to me, Hassan Al Abbas. I am *having* this baby, no matter what. And nothing you can ever say will change my mind.'

The fierce look on her face was unmistakable and for a moment he admired her passion and integrity before indignation reared its head and his face darkened. 'You think that I am suggesting—'

'Don't even say it!' she warned.

Hassan gave an impatient wave of his hand. 'I am not used to being interrupted.'

'Well, I'm not used to having insults hurled at me.

So if you can manage to keep a civil tongue in your head, I promise I won't interrupt you and then we should be fine, shouldn't we?'

His eyes narrowed as he remembered her determination to remove him from her office so that she could continue working and suddenly a solution came to him. Suddenly, he realised exactly how he should handle this. 'We need to decide what we're going to do,' he said.

The use of the word *we* made Ella faintly uneasy. 'I told you, the decision has already been made. I'm having the baby, and I'm perfectly prepared to bring her or him up on my own.'

'But you can't make decisions like that because it isn't just *your* baby,' he said softly. 'This child has royal blood in its veins. Do you have any idea what that means, Ella?'

'How can I? The world of sheikhdom is a mystery to me. Actually, come to think of it, so are you.'

'Oh, I don't think so.' His voice dipped as he ran his eyes over her body. 'I think there are plenty of things about me which are no mystery whatsoever.'

The sensual allusion was obvious and, she suspected, intentional. To Ella's fury, she felt her face grow hot, despite all her best intentions. She'd vowed not to react to him in any way other than a strictly business-like one, and now here she was, colouring up like a naive schoolgirl. 'I don't want to talk about that.'

A mixture of emotions he didn't even want to acknowledge made him want to hurt her. To make her pay for having trapped him, because wasn't that easier than admitting that he had walked right into it? 'What, the sex you couldn't get enough of?'

'But it was the same for you!' she flashed back. 'Wasn't it?'

He met the challenge in her eyes and had to fight down an urgent desire to kiss her. He had been wondering just what it was about her which had made him lose his head—and his body—so completely. Her own amazing body coupled with his own frustration had been obvious contenders, but he realised that her fearlessness was a turn-on too. He'd seen it in the way she'd turned on him in the darkened corridor of the palace at Santina and faced him down. And she was demonstrating it now—her clear blue eyes wide and unafraid, despite the enormity of her situation. 'Yes,' he admitted harshly. 'It was the same for me.'

His words ignited memories she was trying her best to forget. The feeling of being in his arms. The crush of his mouth on hers and the instant flaring of her body in response. Ella tried to ignore the sudden yearning to have him make love to her all over again. *Concentrate on what is real*, she thought as she forced herself to confront her greatest fear and most foolish hope. 'Are you saying you want a hands-on role as father?'

For a moment, Hassan didn't answer. 'I'm saying that's a possibility. But I think it's important that we discuss your needs first.'

Ella blinked in surprise. Was that genuine concern she heard in his voice? 'My needs?' she echoed.

'Well, you have your own business, don't you? I don't know very much about party-planning, but I imagine it must require a lot of hard work and dedication, especially as you're the boss.'

Cautiously, Ella nodded. 'Yes, it does.'

'And some pretty unsociable hours?'

'That's one of the drawbacks,' she agreed, softening in spite of herself, because she would never have believed that he could be quite so understanding.

'And a baby might get in the way of that?'

'Well, ye—' The words died on her lips as she looked into his face and saw that it wasn't concern but calculation she saw in his black eyes. And suddenly, she realised just where this was leading. Suddenly, she realised what a sucker she was for just a few kind words. Was that what her mother had done, over and over again? Fallen under the spell of a man who had treated her like dirt just because he'd uttered a few sweet nothings along the way? The shock of realising that she had very nearly done the same thing made the blood drain from her face.

'My God,' she breathed. 'You are completely and utterly ruthless! I see exactly what you're doing. You're trying to get me to admit that I won't be able to cope with this baby, aren't you?'

'And isn't that the truth?' he challenged, his vow to tread carefully forgotten in his determination to get his own way. 'Have you actually stopped to think about it, about what it might mean to you?'

'Are you crazy? I've thought of nothing else for weeks!'

'But you're planning to carry on working?'

'Of course I am!' Did he have no idea how real people lived their lives? She supposed he didn't. 'It's how I earn my living, Hassan. We weren't all born in palaces and given trust funds while we lay around like pampered princes!'

He gave a short laugh. Oh, the famous myth that all princes were pampered simply because they were princes. If he told her what the reality was, she would never believe it. Instead he leaned forward to emphasise his point, slamming his forefinger into the palm of his hand. 'And while you're "working," Ella, while you're dealing with all the mindless Z-list celebrities and their attendant problems, what will you be doing with our baby? Farming it out to some underqualified child-minder who has no vested interest in its future?'

Heart racing, Ella stared at him. 'That's such an ignorant comment, it doesn't even deserve the dignity of a reply.'

'You think so? Well, how about coming up with an answer to this one? How about when the baby is ill. Who's going to cover for you then? Or are you planning to bring a carrycot into that cramped excuse for a room which you call an office?'

His words were crowding into her mind like a flock of dark birds flapping their demented wings and Ella shook her head as she tried to shake them off. 'I'm not the first woman in the history of the world to contemplate bringing up a child on my own! These are things which can all be worked out.'

'How?' he shot back.

The question caught her off-guard because in truth she hadn't sat down to work out the day-to-day practicalities. 'Okay, so what's the alternative?' she questioned hotly. 'Are you saying you want to take the child off to your desert palace and bring it up as a baby sheikh or whatever it is they call the girl version?'

'It's a sheika, and yes, I can bring up a baby,' he said. 'The way my father brought me up. A child doesn't need a mother in order to survive.'

Ella heard the strange bitterness which had distorted his words and suddenly she realised just where this was leading. She could read the ruthless intent which had darkened his face just as easily as if he'd said the words out loud.

He would take her baby away without a qualm. Take it away to live in some remote desert kingdom and she would never see it again.

Her stomach lurched and pinpricks of sweat broke out on her forehead. 'I think I'm going to be sick,' she croaked.

CHAPTER EIGHT

HASSAN had dealt with sickness before. He'd seen men spill their guts up after battle and afterwards lie grey-faced and sweating. But he'd never witnessed it in a beautiful young woman in her prime and he thought how tiny and frail she suddenly looked. Overwhelmed with remorse at the harshness of his words, he carried her to the tiny bathroom and then held back her hair from her face as she retched. Eventually, she stopped and slumped against his chest, exhausted, her eyes closed.

'I'm sorry,' she said eventually.

Stricken with remorse, he shook his head. 'It is not you who should be sorry, it is me,' he grated. 'I am responsible for your sickness. I should not have said those things to you.'

At this, her eyelashes fluttered open to reveal ice-blue eyes which were slightly bloodshot, and to his astonishment, a faint smile was lifting the corners of her lips.

'Your words *were* rather wounding,' she conceded. 'But not quite powerful enough to induce nausea, Hassan. That's something which happens to lots of pregnant women, no matter what their circumstances.'

'You have been sick before this?' he demanded.

Ella swallowed, feeling much too weak to be able to maintain a stoic attitude. 'Most days.'

'Most days? But this is not good! This is why you are looking so thin and so pale.'

'The doctor says the baby will be fine.'

There was a pause. 'You have seen a doctor?'

Ella knew that she ought to move. That it was bizarre, ridiculous and inappropriate to be lying slumped against the man who had said such cruel things to her. But the stupid thing was that she didn't want to go anywhere. He felt warm and he felt strong. Most important of all, he felt *safe.* 'Seeing a doctor is what normally happens when a woman gets pregnant, Hassan.'

'And who is this doctor?'

'He's my GP from the local health centre and he's very good.'

Hassan tensed, his apprehension eclipsing the sudden realisation that her back was pressing against his groin.

'A local GP cannot be charged with caring for the progeny of the sheikh,' he said, and then saw her eyelids flutter to a close again. 'But this is not the time to talk about it. For now, you need to rest.'

Her protest died on her lips as once again he picked her up and carried her through to her bedroom, though she couldn't miss his faint double take when he saw a series of charcoal drawings she'd done of Izzy lining the walls. They were entitled 'Izzy Dressing' and they showed her sister pulling on various items of clothing. They were less shocking than most things you'd see in a municipal art gallery, but that didn't stop Hassan's mouth from flattening critically.

He put her down on the bed, banking the pillows up behind her, his black eyes raking over her.

'What can I do for you?' he demanded. 'What can I get you to make you feel better?'

Stupidly, she felt like asking him to hold her again. To cradle her in his arms where, for just a brief while, she had felt safe and cosseted. And how pathetic was *that*? She struggled to sit up. 'I don't want anything.'

'Sure?'

The unexpected softness in his voice made her hesitate, especially as her throat felt scorched and dry from all that vomiting. 'There's some flat cola in the fridge.'

His eyes narrowed. 'Flat cola?'

'It helps the sickness.'

'Right.' Grimly, he made his way to her refrigerator, an ancient-looking beast of a thing which contained a lump of cheese, some wilting salad and a bottle of cola, minus the top. His expression was no less thunderous when he took the unappetising brown liquid back to her, and held the glass up to her lips while she sipped from it.

It was an unexpectedly considerate gesture, powerfully intimate, and Ella felt some of her strength returning. 'You make a good nurse,' she joked.

'And you make an appalling patient,' he retorted. 'If you think that you can sustain yourself and a growing baby on that pitiful *excuse* for food in your kitchen.'

'I don't have a lot of time to go shopping,' she defended, and then realised that she had walked into a trap of her own making. 'But all that will change, of course.'

'How?' he demanded. 'Where's the magic wand you're going to wave? Who's going to help you, Ella?'

'My family.' But even to her own ears, the words sounded unconvincing. She knew that Ben would help her in a moment and yet she baulked at the thought of running to him, terrified of disappointing her beloved big brother and becoming a burden to him. Besides, Ben lived on an island which was miles away.

And what of her business—how *was* she going to cope with the day-to-day running of it? Her celebrity clients expected a super-willowy boss, with smiling lips covered in her trademark scarlet gloss. Not some tired and lumbering pregnant woman who wasn't even with the father of her baby, a pregnant woman who was finding it increasingly difficult to stay upright without wanting to fall asleep. Or be sick.

'No, most definitely *not* your family. I am not having this baby influenced by the Jackson family,' said Hassan unequivocably.

Her hackles began to rise. 'You can't stop me.'

No, he couldn't, and he recognised that to try to push her would only make her stubbornly stand her ground. Far better, surely, to appeal to the innate sense of greed which lay at the heart of every woman? Greed which he had seen in many forms ever since his powerful body had reached adulthood and the vast resources of his inheritance had become available to him. He put the half-empty glass of cola on the bedside table and leaned forward by a fraction, seeing her ice-blue eyes widen automatically.

'But what if *I* were to wave the magic wand instead?' he questioned slowly.

'By making yourself disappear from my life? Now that really *would* be a wish come true!'

How indomitable she was, he thought. And what remarkable spirit she would pass on to their child! Unexpectedly, he smiled. 'By listening to reason.'

'Are you trying to tell me that you're a reasonable man?'

'I can be.' He paused. 'What if I arranged for someone to stand in for you at work while you're pregnant? Someone who would ably assist the woman who was staring at me so intently when I came to see you today.'

'Daisy,' she said automatically. 'And I can't afford to just hire someone in.'

'Maybe not, but I can. And not just anyone. The very best in the business—someone of your choosing, of course—can be yours for the taking.'

She stared at him, her heart beginning to race, unable to deny that she was tempted by his offer. How easy it was for him, she thought. He could just chuck money at a problem and the problem would go away. What must it be like, to be that powerful? 'And what's the catch?'

'The catch is that you let me look after you.'

'I know I just said you'd make a good nurse, but I wasn't being serious.'

But even as she attempted the poor joke, Hassan could hear the lack of conviction in her voice. Sensing weakness, he moved in for the kill. 'Think about it, Ella. You can spend your days doing exactly as you please. You can read books you never have time for.

You can relax and watch movies.' His eyes strayed upwards to the drawings of her sister and, again, his mouth flattened. 'You could even do some drawing, if you wanted. Maybe it would be good to have time to do those kinds of things for a change?'

Ella felt temptation grow as she considered his offer. Time to paint? Or to do nothing at all? To lie in bed in the morning until this wretched sickness had passed? She imagined not having to dress for work, to slip on the high heels and slap on the makeup. She'd worked since the age of sixteen and she couldn't imagine *not* working, and yet there was no denying that the idea appealed to her.

But she felt like a bit like a starving stray cat who was too scared to reach out to take the morsels of delicious food which were being offered to her.

'It's very generous of you,' she said slowly.

Hassan allowed himself a charitable smile. 'I can afford to be generous.'

She swallowed. 'And what...you'd come and see me from time to time, would you? Whenever you're in London?'

His eyes narrowed. Surely she had understood the main thrust behind his offer—that in return for rescuing her, she would come under his control? He looked at the question in her eyes. It seemed not. 'But that is not my plan,' he said softly. 'I have a country to run and many pressing matters. We have only just finished fighting a war. I won't be in London and neither will you, for you will fly back to Kashamak with me, just as soon as your replacement can be appointed.'

Ella looked at him blankly. 'Kashamak?' she said faintly.

'The land that I rule which produces fine warriors and great poets,' he said proudly. 'And the child that you carry must know all about their heritage, Ella.' There was a pause. 'And so must you.'

Yet deep down, he suspected she would find his land much too harsh for her Western sensibilities. What if prolonged exposure to Kashamak made her want to escape from its restrictions and return to the freedoms of her old life? What if she discovered that motherhood was not for her?

A sudden and audacious thought occurred to him.

She could leave the child behind. Leave him to care for that child, as his own father had cared for him. Because didn't he know better than anyone that you didn't need a mother in order to survive?

Hassan's heart began to beat with an exultant kind of excitement as he realised what lay within his grasp. That perhaps this was the answer to his prayers. The heir he knew his people wanted and yet which, so far, he had been unwilling to provide, because the idea of marriage had been abhorrent to him. But now he was being forced to marry, wasn't he? And that completely changed the playing field.

Ella watched as his body tensed and wondered what had caused his face to darken like that. 'But I might not want to go and live in Kashamak,' she objected. 'And then what?'

'I think you'll find that you don't really have any choice in the matter,' he snapped, because the alternative was unthinkable, especially now that he had glimpsed the possibilities. The idea of his child being tutored in the ways of the world by the Jackson family would simply not be allowed to happen. He forced his voice to soften as he looked down at her. 'Your welfare is my number-one concern, Ella, and I cannot monitor it if you are thousands of miles away.'

She heard words which sounded as empty as the look in his eyes and a shiver of trepidation whispered its way over her skin. Her welfare was his 'number-one concern,' was it? Sure it was! She didn't believe him. Not for a minute. This felt more about possession than anything else. *His* child and therefore *his* woman.

His hawk-like features looked cruel in that moment, almost triumphant. How she wished she could just pull the bedcovers over her head and make him and all her problems go away.

But he was right. She didn't have a choice. Not really. She was pregnant with the sheikh's baby and she was going to have to accommodate that fact, as were other people. For the first time she thought how this piece of news would go down in Hassan's homeland and she looked up into his flinty eyes.

'Won't your people find it odd if you just turn up with a Western woman who's so obviously pregnant?'

'They would find it completely unacceptable,' he agreed silkily, realising that there was only one solution to their predicament. One which would inevitably mean a deeper association with the outrageous Jackson clan. Instinctively, he baulked against it, but what choice did he have other than to accept it? He looked down into her ice-blue eyes. 'Which is why we must be married immediately.'

Married? Ella stared at him, her heart beginning to beat very fast. 'Are you out of your mind?'

'Not last time I looked.' He saw the tension in her face. 'What's the matter, Ella, were you holding out for Mr Right?'

She thought of her father's multiple marriages and the women whose hearts he had trampled along the way and she shook her head. 'I'm too old to believe in fairy tales,' she said.

His cynical smile mirrored hers. 'Me too. So you see, maybe we are more alike than you think, since neither of us have any illusions to destroy. Maybe that makes us the ideal couple to get married, if the purpose of marriage is to legitimise children. And my country tends to be rather liberal about divorce. If you find living in Kashamak to be unbearable, I will give you your freedom, once the child is born.'

Ella's teeth dug into the fleshy cushion of her bottom lip, because his offer of an easy divorce seemed to make a complete mockery of his marriage proposal. Yet wasn't his suggestion the only thing which made sense in this whole crazy situation? That there was an escape route all mapped out if she chose to take it—and frankly, she couldn't imagine *not* taking it.

It was just his arrogant *certainty* that he could just snap his fingers and she'd fall in with his plans which made her want to rebel. And so did something else—the very real fear that going to a faraway country to live with Hassan would throw up all kinds of new problems. Alone with a man who seemed to despise her… How on earth could she feel comfortable about something like that?

'And what if I refuse?' she challenged quietly. 'What then?'

Hassan stared at her. Was she seriously pitting her will against *his*? It seemed that she was, judging by the sudden determined tilt of her chin, and he forced himself to remember that she was pregnant, and volatile. 'Don't make it hard on yourself, Ella,' he said silkily. 'Why not sit back and let me take care of you?'

His words were like soft but very effective weapons aimed straight at the most vulnerable part of her and Ella felt temptation wash over her. Someone to take care of her. Because when had *that* ever happened before? She thought about the struggle of doing this pregnancy on her own. Of lumbering into work every day on the train and worrying like crazy about money.

And then she thought about this man who had put her in this predicament. She saw the glitter of his black eyes as they observed her. Would it be so terrible to let him take over, to use the abundant power at his fingertips to make her life a little easier? A wave of nausea washed over her and briefly she closed her eyes to let it pass. But it had the effect of emphasising her general weakness and, with a heavy sigh, she nodded. 'Okay,' she said. 'I'll marry you.'

Hassan looked down into her ashen face as he registered her grudging tone and the briefest of smiles glimmered on his lips. Whoever would have predicted it?

That after years of women plotting and scheming to get him to commit, his eventual bride should consent to marry him with such obvious reluctance.

CHAPTER NINE

'So you really *are* called Cinderella?'

Ella had been staring out of the car window at the stark beauty of the desert speeding by, but she turned now to look at the robed figure by her side. *Her new husband.* She might have thought she was in the middle of a particularly bizarre dream were it not for the faint weakness and queasiness she was still experiencing from her pregnancy. But she dredged up a rueful smile from somewhere as she turned to answer Hassan's question. 'I'm afraid I am. Apparently, my father told my mother that giving me such a name meant I'd be bound to marry a prince.'

'Then for once, your father was right,' commented Hassan drily. 'I am rarely surprised, but I certainly was when the registrar read out your full name during the marriage ceremony.'

'I wasn't planning on announcing it,' she admitted, giving a little shrug of her shoulders. 'It's something I tend to keep quiet about, but the registrar insisted that I declare it.'

'You must have been teased about it a lot at school,' he observed.

'Oh, being a Jackson was enough to ensure *that.*

Having a ridiculous Christian name didn't really make any difference.'

But her airy assertion didn't quite ring true and Hassan surveyed her with thoughtful eyes. He'd dismissed her as nothing but a playful flirt when she'd first introduced herself with the storybook name. He'd never have dreamt in a million years that she was telling the truth. And yet it had fitted his stereotypical views of women to think of her as a sexy and teasing minx, rather than this rather solemn mother-to-be who now wore his wedding band. He let his gaze drift over the paleness of her skin and felt a sudden beat of anxiety. 'The car is not too bumpy for you? You don't feel sick?'

'No sicker than I was feeling back in London, and it's nothing to do with the car, or the road. Why, it's so smooth that you'd hardly believe we were speeding along in the middle of a desert!'

'Probably because you imagined the roads of Kashamak would be primitive dirt tracks, potted with holes and barely passable because of camels? Didn't you once say something predictable about camels?'

'Maybe I was a little guilty of that,' she said as she stared down at the shiny new wedding ring on her finger, still dazed by the speed of everything that had happened. Still unable to believe that the dark-faced man sitting at her side really *was* her husband, as well as the father of her child.

Had she been out of her mind to agree to their hasty marriage, or simply too dazed by sickness and general worries to protest about the future? And hadn't her decision to wed him been made easier by his offer of an 'easy' divorce, should she want one?

She sat back against the soft leather of the car seat. 'I wasn't sure what to expect when I got here, but so far everything has defied all my expectations.'

The insights as to how her new life would be had begun the moment she'd boarded the luxury jet on a private airfield just north of London. The flight had been seamless and further than she'd ever flown before. With mainland Europe far behind them, they'd skirted the edges of the beautiful Caspian Sea before coming in to land at the airport in Samaltyn, the capital city of Kashamak.

Protocol had been discreet on the plane, which had been empty save for them and the crew members who outnumbered them. But the moment they'd landed and Ella had heard the national anthem being played, she had realised that she was actually in the company of a real-live king.

While she—unbelievable as it seemed—was his new queen. A queen kitted out in lavish silks which covered every bit of available flesh, except for her face and hands.

Their marriage had taken place in the Kashamak Embassy in central London, with only two diplomats as their witnesses and no advance publicity given out, not even to their respective families. Hassan had been adamant he didn't want an international frenzy with swarms of paparazzi clustering around to take photos of the sheikh's new Western queen.

But Ella knew this wasn't the only reason he had insisted on no fuss and why a quiet statement about their union had been issued only this morning, just as they were about to board their jet. She suspected he was terrified of all the negative publicity which always surrounded the Jackson family. And if that *was* the case, then she was forced to concede that he might be right.

She could just imagine how her family might have sabotaged their wedding day. Her father boasting that his daughter was marrying one of the most powerful men in the Middle East. Her mother playing her habitual doormat role beside him. And Izzy—heaven forbid—trying to sing her congratulations.

But Ella was also afraid that one of her sisters might have discovered the truth behind her bright smile and realised the heavy burden she was carrying. That Hassan was only marrying her to stamp his mark of possession on their unborn baby.

And now they were travelling in a sleek air-conditioned car towards Hassan's palace, on roads which were as flat as millponds. She felt…well, she felt as displaced as most women would feel if they were newly pregnant and leaving behind everything they knew. *But most women in her position would have the comfort of knowing that they were loved and desired, instead of regarded as some sort of royal incubator.*

Her actions instinctively mirroring her turbulent emotions, she moved her hand to let it rest on her stomach.

'You are experiencing discomfort?' questioned Hassan instantly. 'Some kind of pain?'

She shook her head, because she had decided that she was going to be strong. She wasn't going to start whingeing every time she had a little ache or wave of sickness. 'Hassan, I'm fine.'

He stared at the fingers which were curled protectively over her stomach, wondering when this would all start to feel real. As if it was happening to him and not to someone else. He stared at the unfamiliar bump and tried to make sense of it. 'The baby is kicking?'

'No, not yet.'

'When?'

Her fingers tightened around the still unfamiliar swell. 'Any day now, I hope.'

'How can you know all these things?'

His dark, gleaming eyes were curious and Ella thought at that moment how gorgeous he looked, and yet how unreachable too. His traditional Kashmakian robes made him look so darkly foreign and yet the flowing silk emphasised the honed body beneath, mocking her with memories of that snatched and forbidden night they'd spent together. The first and only time they'd made love…

Blocking out the sudden flare of desire which shimmered over her skin and the inevitable questions that raised, she attempted to answer his question.

'There's a chart which you can download from the internet and it tells you all the things you can expect,' she explained carefully. 'Movement starts around sixteen weeks.'

'And will you let me feel my child when it kicks, Ella?' he questioned suddenly. 'Will you let me lay my hand on your belly so that I can feel it move?'

Despite the cool of the air conditioning, Ella's cheeks grew heated at the intimacy of his question.

Their night of passion had happened so long ago that sometimes it seemed as if it was nothing but a distant dream. And the more time passed, the more unreal it seemed. Because there had been no revisiting of that passion since that night. No sense that he wanted to touch her in any way at all.

So if he laid his hand on her stomach, would that start her yearning for a greater intimacy altogether? Did he still want her in that way? she wondered.

'Yes, of course you can,' she answered quietly, knowing that she couldn't possibly refuse him. Not just because he was the baby's father, but because he'd done so much to help her. And for once in her life she had just sat back and let him help with a passivity which she put down to her pregnancy and to the accompanying nausea which still hit her in waves.

Somehow, Hassan had produced a clutch of women who were eager to step into her shoes at work and Ella had interviewed every one of them. And right now, back in England, Daisy was working quite happily alongside her replacement, while the business was ticking along just fine.

But there were more things to occupy her mind other than the business she'd left behind. Ahead she could see an enormous and elaborate pair of golden gates dazzling in the sunshine and, beyond those, neat lines of palm trees bordering a bright rectangle of water. A vast creamy-gold building rose up in the distance—a structure so wide and so grand that, once again, she wanted to pinch herself to convince herself she wasn't dreaming.

They had reached the royal palace at last, and suddenly all her doubts came skimming to the surface, making her stomach churn with fear. Had she forgotten who she was? Just one of the notorious Jacksons whose father had kept the British press entertained for years. How could she go from being mocked and ridiculed to wearing a crown on her head and carrying it off with any degree of confidence?

'Hassan, I can't do this,' she croaked. 'What if your people won't accept me?'

Hearing the crack in her voice, Hassan turned, trying to see her as others would see her for the first time. She was wearing an exquisite Kashamak robe in bridal colours of deep scarlet and ornamental gold. Her hair was covered by a golden veil and her eyes were ringed heavily with kohl pencil. Even her scarlet lipstick had been replaced by a glimmering rose-pink, which made her mouth look so much softer.

She had told him that she wanted her first appearance in his land to be as traditional as possible and he respected her for her thoughtfulness. And she looked, he thought with a sudden wrench of longing, absolutely beautiful. A delectable mixture of East and West, she seemed to represent the very best of both their cultures.

'Your appearance is faultless,' he said slowly. 'You need not concern yourself on that score. And as king, my people will accept what I tell them to accept.'

His reassuring words gave her a moment of comfort and she clung to it, as a child would to a security blanket. 'And what about your brother, Kamal?'

He flicked her a glance. 'What about him?'

'I'm…looking forward to meeting him.'

His smile was bland. 'That won't be happening immediately, I'm afraid, since he has decided to ride off into the desert in order to escape the rigours of court life.'

Ella swallowed. Or to escape from having to meet *her*? she wondered. 'Didn't you say that he's been running the country while you were away fighting the war? Won't he mind handing back the reins to you?' She hesitated. 'Power can be addictive stuff.'

He gave a hard smile. 'Kamal is going to have to get used to a lot of changes,' he said. 'And to build a new role for himself. Because, of course, of much greater significance to him than my returning to rule is the fact that you are carrying my child.' *And hadn't he always led his brother to believe that he had no desire to procreate? Would Kamal think that he had broken his word and thus changed both their destinies?*

Ella's voice broke into his troubled thoughts.

'And that child will one day inherit?' she asked.

'Only if it is a son.' His black eyes bored into her. '*Is* it a son, Ella? Do you know that already?'

She felt colour rising in her cheeks as his gaze washed over her. 'No, no, I don't. They couldn't tell on the first scan and I…'

'What?'

She shook her head, hating the way that he made her feel like a butterfly pinned onto a piece of cardboard. 'I don't want to know!' she said fiercely. 'I don't want that kind of pressure spoiling the pregnancy in any way. I don't want you being pleased if it's a boy and your brother being pleased if it's a girl, so that I'll end up feeling tugged both ways. I want the surprise of *not* knowing. Otherwise it will be like knowing what all your Christmas presents are before you actually get around to unwrapping them.'

For a moment, he smiled. 'I'm afraid we don't celebrate Christmas in Kashamak,' he offered drily.

'Well, your birthday presents, then.'

'I wouldn't really know about that either.'

She stared at him in disbelief. 'You're not trying to tell me you never had any birthday presents?'

'So what if I didn't?' He shrugged. 'My father was too busy for that kind of thing. Sometimes he remembered, sometimes not. It wasn't important.'

Ella's heart gave a funny little flip. Of course it was important, especially to a child. It was the one day a year when you could guarantee that all the attention would be focused on you. You got the feeling that you were loved and cared for. Even when money was at its tightest her mother had always managed to pull together *some* sort of celebration. And it couldn't have been easy for her, she realised suddenly. Not easy at all.

'And what about your mother, didn't she want a birthday cake for her little boy?'

Silently, he cursed her overemotional use of language. Was that deliberate? Was she trying to get under his skin, in the way that women always did? 'My mother wasn't around,' he clipped out.

'What happened to her?' Ella's voice softened. 'You never mention her, Hassan. Did she…did she die?'

The knuckles of his fists gleamed white as Hassan clenched his hands over his silk-clad thighs. 'No, she didn't die—at least, not then. She left us to find a different kind of life, and I don't particularly want to talk about it. Especially not now at such a significant moment. Look, here are my advisers and staff come out to greet us. Prepare yourself, Ella, for I am sure you know how important first impressions are.'

Hearing the finality in his voice as he halted the discussion about his childhood, Ella straightened her golden veil with trembling fingers. She certainly remembered her first impression of *him.* How his dark and proudly arrogant beauty had seemed to call out to something deep inside her. How for one blissful night she thought she'd found it, only to have it swept away by his callous desertion of her. Had that been just an illusion? she wondered. And had she been guilty of imagining a special bond where none existed, as a way of justifying her own wanton behaviour?

The powerful car drew to a halt and her memories melted away in the presence of a practical dilemma. Because how on earth did you prepare yourself to face people as their brand-new queen?

'Do they know I'm pregnant?' she asked.

At this he gave an odd kind of smile. 'Of course not, though it is fairly obvious to all but the most careless observer. But you need not concern yourself with that, Ella. Don't you know what they say about royalty? Never complain and never explain. There will be no need for any kind of announcement. Many of my people will not realise the good news until a child is presented to them, for you will largely be hidden from view.'

Hidden from view?

What the hell did *that* mean?

His words sent feelings of alarm skittering over her

skin but there wasn't time to demand further explanation because the door to the car was being opened and a warm blast of fragrant air hit her. Ella exited the car as gracefully as she could—not an easy move, given that her beautiful gown was so jewel-encrusted that it weighed a ton.

Slowly, she walked along two lines of assembled people, where the advisers were exclusively male and wore subdued versions of Hassan's robes. The only women present were servants and they lowered their eyes deferentially as she walked along the line, shyly uttering the Kashamak greeting she'd been practising for days.

There was so much to take in. High ceilings and marble floors, the glimmer of gold and the glitter of crystal. Was this how her sister Allegra had felt when she'd first arrived in Alex's royal palace? Blown away by the sense of history and tradition? And the wealth, of course. Only this was the real thing. Not the kind she'd known when she was growing up, when one minute they'd all be driving around in a gold limousine and the next hiding from the bailiffs.

This was rock-solid wealth. Enduring and sustaining. Money like this could totally influence your thinking and behaviour. And yet, this was their child's heritage, she realised. All this splendour and beauty was his or hers by birth—and she did not have the right to deny their baby that.

'Clearly you approve?' Hassan had watched with interest the movement of her ice-blue eyes as they quickly assessed her surroundings. Was she silently adding up his worth and realising that never again would she want for money?

'It's beautiful,' she breathed. 'Absolutely beautiful.'

Briefly, he found himself wondering whether he should have taken his lawyer's advice and made her sign a prenuptial agreement. But something about that action had made him baulk. It had seemed inherently wrong to ask that of the mother of his child. No matter how outrageous her demands for any divorce settlement, he could easily afford it. And a woman who was satisfied with her pay-out would be less likely to cause trouble in the future….

'So…you must be tired after the long journey,' he said. 'Would you like to see your quarters?'

'My…*quarters*?' Ella's smile was uncertain. 'Um, you've left the army now, Hassan.'

'Forgive me.' His answering smile concealed a faint confusion, an unknown feeling of being out of his depth. Who cared *what* he called it, the detail was surely insignificant? Usually, he would have gone straight off to long meetings with aides and ministers, followed by a hard ride on one of his horses. But now the comforting familiarity of his routine had been broken by a woman with rose-pink lips and ice-blue eyes.

His wife.

If it was anyone else, he would have assigned a servant to show her around. But because it was Ella and she was pregnant and therefore vulnerable, he found himself in the unheard-of position of being her guide. *And for the first time in his life, he felt out of his depth.*

'I will show you to your suite of rooms. Does that sound better?'

'*My* suite?' She looked at him in surprise. For weeks, she'd been psyching herself up for married life. She'd vacillated between wondering if she was crazy to go through with it, or whether it was the only sane choice. But once she'd decided to marry Hassan, one comforting thought had remained to sustain her. At least sex with her new husband was guaranteed to be amazing. He'd shown her that she could experience pleasure in his arms, and the truth was that she couldn't wait to sample it again. She edged him a tentative smile. 'But surely we'll be sharing a suite, as a married couple?'

Hassan shook his head, wiping out the tempting thoughts provoked by the soft curve of her lips. 'It is not the tradition, no, not here. It dates back from the days when a monarch always had to be ready to go to war and did not want to disturb his wife if he left for battle in the middle of the night. So his isolation was a necessity, rather than a luxury.'

Ella's heart missed a beat. 'You're joking?'

'No, I am not. I am simply abiding by tradition, as well as giving you the opportunity to have some private space of your own.' He saw the way her blue eyes had clouded, but for the hundredth time, he told himself it was better this way. Better for both of them. For a divorce would be far simpler if there had been no intimacy. His voice gentled by a fraction. 'My culture is very different from the one you've grown up in, Ella, and you'll need to accept that if you want to find any kind of contentment here.'

Contentment? Did he think she was going to be

content if she was going to be locked away like a nun without even the warm comfort of her new husband by her side? She stared at him, daring herself to voice the truth. 'So we aren't going to be a proper married couple?'

Almost reluctantly, Hassan let his eyes drift over her. With the golden veil framing her pale face he thought how lovely she looked, like some fragile, shimmering statue. In that moment, he could have pulled her close to him and drunk in her exquisite beauty with a passionate kiss. But something stopped him and that something was logic. This was nothing but a marriage of convenience, made with the sole purpose of legitimising their baby. Much better by far to keep their relationship on a formal footing.

'But we aren't a proper married couple, are we, Ella?' he questioned, his harsh tone subduing the sexual hunger which had flared inside him. 'We were never intended to be. And I think it best if we don't complicate this already difficult situation by pretending to be something we're not.'

Ella felt his words rip through her like a chill wind and she stared at him in dismay, realising how isolated her life was going to be if Hassan was planning on distancing himself from her.

Well, she certainly wasn't going to *beg* him to sleep with her! Biting back her hurt, she accompanied him along the wide expanse of marble corridor, wanting to ask him why the hell he hadn't told her all this *before* he'd made her his bride.

Because he *couldn't* have told her, that was why. If he'd given her any intimation of how constricted her life would be in his country then she would have refused to come. No amount of money or the promise of a quick divorce would have tempted her to a life of virtual imprisonment. She would have found some other way to support herself because she would have *had* to.

To all intents and purposes, Hassan had deceived her. But that was now irrelevant. She couldn't change what had happened. All she could do was react to it. And she would do what she had done all her life, no matter what fate had thrown at her. She would adapt to circumstances and she would make the best of them.

But her determination wavered as Hassan informed her that dinner would be at eight and that a servant would come to collect her.

The door closed behind him and she was left alone in the gilded suite. She looked up at the glitter of the crystal chandelier and breathed in the deep scent of the roses which had been crammed into beautiful golden vases. It all looked so perfect, but so unreal. And it *felt* unreal too. As if someone had put her down in the middle of a film set and if she pushed too hard she might discover that the walls were made of cardboard.

Another wave of sickness washed over her and quickly she lay down on the bed, clutching one of the brocade cushions to her stomach as she tried to fight against a tide of tears.

CHAPTER TEN

ANOTHER day in paradise.

Ella stared out of the window which had just been unshuttered by one of the sweet maids whose job it was to attend her. The early-morning scent of flowers wafted fragrance into the room and vied with the perfume of the jasmine tea which stood on the filigree cabinet beside her large bed.

Leaning back against the feathery plumpness of the pillows, she contemplated what the new day might bring. Outside, there was a vast swimming pool which she could use any time she wanted. The beautiful gardens were enormous and varied, with plenty of shaded paths for her to walk along. Benches were positioned at eye-catching vantage points where she could stop to read a book from the palace's vast and comprehensive library. Anything Ella wanted, she could have.

Except it wasn't quite like that.

The one thing she really wanted constantly eluded her.

She wanted her husband.

She wanted to relive the passion they'd shared that night back in Santina, when she'd tasted pleasure for the first time in her life. And surely as his wife she was entitled to that?

The sickness she'd experienced had now passed and she realised that she hadn't been herself when she'd agreed to this marriage. He had asked her—or rather, *told* her—that she would be his wife when she had been at her most vulnerable. Still reeling from the discovery of the baby and weakened by nausea, she had allowed Hassan to take command.

But something had changed. Now that she felt better, it seemed as if she had got some of the old Ella back, and then some. She was filled with a new vigour, buzzing with energy and life. And not only was she growing increasingly frustrated at the celibate state of her marriage, she was determined to do something about it. So what if she was only destined to be here for months. Couldn't they at least be *pleasurable* months?

Had the desire Hassan felt for her disappeared? Ella didn't think so. She may not have been the most experienced woman in the world, but she had definitely seen the hard gleam of his eyes sometimes when they were alone at dinner. Hadn't she once noticed his big body tense when she reached forward to pluck a ripe damson from the heap of fruit piled in a shallow dish? And sit there perfectly still for a moment or two afterwards, as if he was composing himself? No, Hassan certainly wasn't immune to her, no matter how much he'd like to be.

The strangest thing was that once she had allowed herself to acknowledge that what she was feeling was sexual frustration, the feeling just grew and grew. It became so that it dominated her thoughts. So that every time she looked into Hassan's hawk-like features, all she could remember was his helpless look of abandon as he plunged deep inside her body.

She wanted him.

She wanted him badly.

And she realised that nobody was going to make it happen except her.

Quietening the voice in her head which asked if she wasn't crazy to consider seducing such a proud and worldly man as Hassan, she set about her plan.

Piecing together fragments of things she'd read in magazines and books back home in England, she waited until Saturday evening, because she'd learnt that Saturday was one of her husband's lightest days, in terms of royal duties. And that he often lay in bed late on a Sunday…

Dressing carefully in a filmy azure gown which made her eyes look intensely blue, she spent ages on her hair and her makeup. Not too much makeup, because she'd also learnt that where Hassan was concerned, less was more. The ebony sweep of her lashes and rose-pink glimmer of her mouth was flattering but very natural, so that she might almost have been born that way.

As she joined him in the dining room, she was filled with a nervous kind of excitement, and a sudden realisation of what she was about to do made her momentarily reconsider whether she was being sensible. What if he rejected her?

As he rose to greet her, she heard the soft swish of his silken robes and once again she remembered the magnificent body which lay beneath. Swallowing down her fears, she quickly replaced them with determination. She would not *let* him reject her!

A servant poured iced water into her goblet and began to serve the meal, but Ella barely paid it any attention. She pushed various delicious slithers of neglected food around her golden plate and tried not to stare at her husband's dark and thoughtful face.

'You're not eating much,' Hassan observed suddenly.

'Aren't I?' she questioned innocently.

'No.' He studied her through the flickering light of the countless candles which illuminated the gilded room and thought how much she bloomed as every day passed. And what hell it was to resist the temptation of taking her to his bed…

With an effort, he forced his attention back to her lacklustre appetite. 'Are you displeased with the fare which my chefs have slaved over all day in order to impress the sheikh's new bride?'

'The food is delicious. As always.'

'So why haven't you touched it?'

'Because I'm not…' Her words tailed off as nerves began to get the better of her. How could she possibly seduce a man who showed no sign of wanting to be seduced, despite the fact that they were newlyweds?

She wondered what had happened to the hungry hunter who had dragged her to bed on the night of the engagement party. Maybe he was one of those men who only enjoyed sex with a woman he didn't know. Maybe he shied away from that whole intimacy thing. Or was turned off by the fact she was pregnant.

Or maybe he just didn't fancy her any more.

Her pulse rocketed at the thought of tackling such a daunting mission. That she, who had never seduced anyone, should be taking on one of the world's great lovers. Yet Ella wasn't easily defeated. There were many disadvantages to being a Jackson, but one thing it gave you was determination—and grit.

'Not what?' he prompted.

She pushed away her dish more heavily than she'd intended and leaned back against the brocade cushions. 'I'm not very hungry,' she said.

Hassan felt a pulse began to flicker at his temple. 'You need to…eat,' he said unsteadily, trying to ignore the fact that the position she'd now adopted meant that her breasts were looking especially lush and inviting. And hadn't he been resolutely trying to avoid thinking about her breasts, or her lips, or indeed any part of her which reminded him of thrusting deep into her body?

Ella shifted her position a little, pleased to see that the blue silk of her robe was now clinging to her thighs like melted butter. And that Hassan seemed transfixed by the movement. She slanted him a smile, telling herself there was nothing to be gained from a lack of courage. 'I keep thinking of you, asleep nearby.'

'Do you?' He wondered what she'd say if he told her that he had been getting precious little sleep of late. That oblivion stayed tantalisingly out of reach as he lay there imagining the silken touch of her skin and the enticing curves of her body.

'Mmm. And sometimes it gets so hot.'

Did that mean she slept naked? An unstoppable image of her milky thighs and rose-tipped breasts crystallised in his mind and Hassan almost sliced the top of his thumb with the knife he had been using to peel a peach. With trembling fingers, he put both down. 'The palace is air-conditioned,' he growled.

'I know it is, but sometimes I turn it off because it's noisy. And…' Oh, for heaven's sake! Ella winced. What kind of a seduction was *this* if all they were doing was talking about the wretched air conditioning? 'And I wish you were there with me. I'd like that.' She hesitated as she looked straight into his eyes and drew a deep breath. 'In fact, I'd like that very much.'

Hassan tensed as the innocent longing of her words cut through him in a way that the most seasoned seduction could never have done. He felt the tight, hard spring of an erection and silently cursed her. 'That isn't a good idea,' he said thickly.

'Why not? What's stopping us?'

He shook his head. A fear of intimacy, that was what was stopping them. Or rather, stopping *him*. And a very real fear of how such intimacy could complicate this strange marriage of theirs. Should he tell her that he saw nothing but danger if they succumbed, that sex could sometimes cast a dark and distorting spell? But how could he tell her anything when she was pushing back her dark, glossy hair and he was imagining it tumbling down over her naked breasts?

'Ella,' he ground out.

'What?' she whispered, thrilled to see his formidable mask drop for once, to reveal the man beneath. To suddenly see the hard-faced desert sheikh with all the vulnerabilities and doubts of any other person.

With an effort of will which seemed only a little

easier than the time he'd had to endure a full day's ride without fresh water to sustain him, Hassan stood.

'It has been a long day for both of us,' he bit out. 'Come, I will escort you to your room.'

Ella could have wept with disappointment as she realised that the formidable mask was back in place. It hadn't worked and she had no one to blame but herself. All she'd done was to stumble out her pathetic little desire to have him sleep with her. Shouldn't she have been a bit bolder than that? Reached out and *touched* him maybe? Wasn't that what women usually did when they were trying to seduce a man?

What had seemed like a brilliant idea at the time now seemed like complete madness. Once again, she had simply reinforced all his awful prejudices about her and her family with her attempt at seduction, only she couldn't even do *that* properly.

'Very well,' she said stiffly, rising to her feet and waving away the hand he extended to assist her. Did he think she was some kind of invalid?

In smouldering silence she walked alongside him through marbled corridors which were open on one side to the scented courtyard gardens. She heard the soft movement of their flowing robes and the sweet, high trill of a bird she thought might be a nightingale. It seemed almost painfully beautiful and yet she could take no pleasure in it. All she could feel was a terrible emptiness inside, and an underlying ache that he no longer seemed to find her attractive as a woman.

The journey to her room seemed to take forever and she found herself wondering how she was going to be able to endure such an empty and lonely existence, knowing that there was no hope it would ever change.

'Here we are,' he said abruptly as he stopped outside the door to her suite. 'I'll leave you here.'

'Yes.' She looked up at him, surprised by the ravaged look on his face. What had put that terrible bleakness in those eyes of his? she wondered. Had *she*? Had her failed attempt to seduce him reminded him that she shouldn't even *be* here? That she wouldn't be here were it not for the baby? 'Hassan, those things I said at dinner…I, well, I shouldn't have said them. I shouldn't have come on to you like that.'

There was silence for a moment, and when he spoke, his voice sounded as if it was being half strangled out of him.

'I don't want to hurt you, Ella,' he ground out.

She looked at him in confusion. How could he hurt her any more than she was already hurting from him pushing her away? 'I don't understand,' she whispered.

At that moment she looked so damned soft that Hassan felt the unfamiliar prickle of guilt. Usually he used women before they could use him and he had no compunction about doing so. But Ella was different. Even putting her fragility aside, what if deep down she had expectations of him which he could never honour? What if she expected him to be like other men, to feel the things which women wanted men to feel? Could he really bear to crush her hopes and her dreams when she realised that his words had been true. That his heart *was* cold. That it would be easier to facilitate an end to this marriage if they had not grown close through sex.

He made one last appeal as he looked down into the

rose-pink gleam of her lips. 'Don't you realise that this is going to complicate everything?'

'What is?'

'This is,' he ground out. *'This!'*

She honestly didn't realise it was coming until he pulled her into his arms and started kissing her with a fierce urgency which instantly set her on fire. Her arms snaked up round his neck and she clung to him, almost wanting to sob aloud with joy. So he *did* want her—and judging by the tension in his powerful body, he wanted her as badly as she wanted him.

She wondered whether this wasn't a bit public, standing, making out in the corridor of the darkened palace, until she remembered that they were newly-weds. This is exactly what they were *supposed* to be doing, she thought exultantly as he pushed open the door to her suite and pulled her inside.

His hands were shaking and so was his voice as he pulled his mouth away from hers and cradled her face in his palms. 'I don't know how gentle I can be.'

'You don't have to be *gentle.*'

'You're carrying my baby, Ella.'

She turned her head so that her lips brushed against his fingers. 'Well, unless you were planning to tie me up and suspend me from the ceiling…'

'Stop it.' For a moment he bit back unexpected laughter as he ran his fingers through her hair so that the glorious waves of her red-brown hair tumbled free. 'How about if we take it very slowly this time?'

'I'm not sure that I can,' she whispered.

He wasn't sure that he could either, but he would make sure that he was careful. He led her over to the bed and slowly peeled the silken robe from her body. And this was a first too. He'd never undressed a woman who was wearing his own traditional robes and it seemed to add another dimension to the surreal aspect of what was taking place. It was as if all his certainties had been shaken up and scattered haphazardly, like a handful of dice thrown onto a gaming table. And everything was up for grabs. Including his blushing wife.

Clad in exquisite lingerie, her lashes half shaded her blue eyes as she watched his reaction. The cami-knickers clung to her slender hips and the silk bra caressed the curve of her breasts. Eyes narrowing, he studied the pale, creamy colour of the garments which looked distinctly bridal.

'Did you choose this especially for me?' he questioned unevenly, curving his finger around the lace edge of her bra.

'Of course I did. I went out shopping especially.' Hadn't she slunk out almost shamefacedly to buy it in the few hours available before their rushed wedding? Wondering if she was being a hypocrite by purchasing brand-new underwear for a wedding which felt distinctly empty. Yet now Ella was pleased she'd done it. It had been worth all those doubts just to see the dark fire which had shifted the emptiness from his eyes. 'It's called a trousseau. It's what every bride should wear on her honeymoon. I know that, traditionally, it's supposed to be white, but I don't really qualify for white, do I?'

'Who cares about that?' he questioned roughly.

'You mean you don't?'

He shook his head. He hadn't seen her body since the night of the party and it had changed. Of course it had. The breasts were fuller and her belly curved over the edge of her lace panties. He gave a groan which was part lust and part admiration as he let his fingers curl over the gentle swell, because beneath her silken robes, he hadn't realised how big she was getting. Did all men experience a rush of possessive pride when they witnessed their child growing in a woman's belly? he wondered.

'You look beautiful,' he husked as he pushed her down onto the bed, quickly removing his own robes before joining her and pulling a throw over them both.

'I'm not cold,' she murmured as they were cocooned in the light concealment of silk.

'No?' He kissed the soft flesh of her shoulder. 'Then why are you shivering?'

'You know very well why,' she whispered as she curled her hand around his neck and brought his head down to kiss her. It was the second assertive thing she'd done that evening and it seemed to liberate Hassan from his porcelain-like treatment of her as he opened her lips with the thrust of his tongue.

Ella could feel the warmth of his breath mingling with hers. His kiss was like a drug—one taste and she was hooked. Deeply and passionately she kissed him back, her fingers kneading at the silken skin which played over the muscles of his back. And then he began to touch her.

Everywhere.

She closed her eyes. This was unbelievable. Even better than last time. She could feel the relentless heat building inside her as he unclipped her bra to free her aching breasts, capturing first one and then the other in the hot, moist cavern of his mouth. She was restless and gasping by the time he slid her panties off. She knew he'd said he was going to take it slowly, but *really...*

'Keep still,' he urged her mockingly.

'I *can't*!'

Concerned that his weight might press on the baby, he brought her instead to sit on top of him, positioning the tip of his erection against her slick, moist folds. But even as he gripped her hips to slowly guide himself inside her, he was aware of a sudden sense of discovery. Of something unfamiliar happening to him. He felt the warmth of her thighs as they pressed into his sides and he shuddered as she pushed her hips forward to make him go even deeper. And then he realised what it was. That this was the first time he'd ever had sex with a pregnant woman, and the first time he'd never worn protection.

And it felt…

He closed his eyes. It felt *unbelievable.* He'd overheard men talking about the joys of 'riding bareback' while knowing that, for him, it would never be an option. Because royal seed was too precious to squander by careless lust or an inability to wait. But now he was experiencing it for the first time in his life, and it felt almost unbearably intimate as he thrust deep inside her. Skin on skin. Her slick heat against his hard heat.

'I'm not hurting you?' he managed.

Ella shook her head, barely able to speak, realising that she had wanted this so much. To feel this close to him again. To experience the pleasure which only he had ever given her. 'I'm going to…going to…'

'I can see that for myself,' he murmured, watching as her head tipped back with helpless joy. She made a moaning sound as she came, a low note of uninhibited pleasure which initiated the beginning of his own orgasm. Holding tightly onto her hips, he felt the powerful spasms which swept him up in a mindless spill he never wanted to end.

Afterwards, his head fell back against the pillow and he felt as drained and as elated as a battle-weary soldier. Yet even as his hand encircled her waist to draw her closer and he found himself breathing in the raw scent of sex, he found himself thinking that this could get addictive. Dangerously addictive. The combined warmth of their damp skin made their bodies seemed glued together and he found himself absently kissing the tangle of her hair as long, silent minutes ticked by.

He must have slept more deeply than usual because when he opened his eyes, sunlight was filtering through the open shutters and the early-morning scent of roses was powerfully intoxicating. For a moment he didn't remember where he was, but as he turned to see the sleeping form of Ella beside him, it all came back. Her shy and stumbled entreaty at dinner. A hesitant seduction which had proved inordinately irresistible.

Yawning, he thought that his senses had never felt so finely tuned, nor so richly satiated. Last night had been, he realised, the most erotic experience of his life.

More than that, he felt a rare moment of contentment which allowed him to push away the nagging questions which were hovering at the back of his mind.

He knew that there were a million things he should be doing. He should rouse himself and move away from the warm comfort of this bed….

But instead, he picked up a handful of Ella's hair, watching as it fell in satin tendrils across his chest before bending his lips to her ear. 'Awake?' he questioned lazily.

She wriggled and smiled against the pillow. 'I am now.'

He guided her hand towards his aching groin. 'You are the most amazing lover, do you know that?'

Ella froze as her fingers encountered the steely shaft of his erection, and in the cold light of day, fear began to run through her veins. What if he now expected her to run through a repertoire of sexual skills—skills she didn't have, and which would leave him sorely disappointed?

Before, she had not cared about his good opinion of her but suddenly it became vital that he should know the truth. 'I'm not the person you think I am,' she said, pulling her hand away from him. Even though she saw his eyes narrow with disappointment, he needed to realise that she wasn't the sexual expert he imagined her to be. Not some uber-experienced party girl with dozens of men in her past and a long list of lovers she could barely remember.

Hassan winced, wondering why women always chose precisely the wrong moment to pour out their feelings. But he was in no position to move. He registered the heavy aching at his groin and realised he was in no position to do anything except… 'And what kind of person is that?' he questioned unsteadily.

She drew in a deep breath. 'I don't make a habit of seducing men.'

'I'd kind of worked that out for myself, Ella.'

'You had?'

'Mmm.' He moved his hand between her legs. 'Last night you came over as sweet, rather than seasoned.'

She wondered if that was a good thing or a bad thing. In fact, it was difficult to wonder anything when he was stroking her like that. 'Up…up until that night of the party, I'd…well, I'd never behaved like that before.'

'I'm very pleased to hear it,' he replied gravely.

'I'd only ever had a relationship with one other person. And I went out with him for ages before we had sex.' Through her growing waves of pleasure, she met the question in his eyes, admitting to herself for the first time that she'd been scared of sex. She'd seen from the example set by her own parents what fools men and women could make of themselves in its pursuit. 'When eventually we did it, I…well, I tried my best. But I never…never…' She shook her head, the words sticking in her throat.

'You never had an orgasm before me?' he guessed as he remembered the way she'd clung to him that first time. And suddenly it all made sense. The breathless little words which had sounded almost like gratitude as she had bucked wildly in his arms.

'Right.' She looked into his eyes, wary now that she had given too much away. Wouldn't a man like him hate such transparency? 'So I misled you. I'm not the woman you thought I was. Are you angry with me, Hassan?'

His mouth twitched. 'Absolutely furious,' he said.

'Seriously?'

His laugh was low as his fingertip thrummed against her heated flesh. 'Oh, Ella,' he murmured. 'Don't you know that it's every man's fantasy to be the first person to awaken a woman in that way? I *like* the fact that I am the only man to have shown you true pleasure. That everything you learn will spring from my lips and my loins.' His voice dipped into a throaty murmur. 'Shall I show you how good it feels when a man tastes a woman?'

Shyly, she nodded, her cheeks growing warm as he began to move his lips slowly down over her body. And in that moment she thought she'd just discovered the *real* danger of sex. Because when a man made her feel this good… When his tongue was licking her in places where she'd never imagined being licked… It was easy to start imagining what it might be like if Hassan loved her.

And that was *never* going to happen.

CHAPTER ELEVEN

'HASSAN.' Ella paused long enough to ensure that she had her husband's complete attention. 'I can't spend much more time doing this.'

Hassan looked up from his newspaper. The light was flooding into the breakfast room and glimmering off the red-brown curls which spilled over Ella's shoulders. The silk robe she wore was loose and flowing but the unmistakable swell of her belly drew the eye like nothing else. And the by-now familiar sense of wonder settled over him as he surveyed the blossoming body of his wife.

The passing weeks had made obvious the unspoken secret within the palace—that the queen was with child. And Hassan couldn't help but question if that was the reason for his brother's continuing absence from court life. It was unlike Kamal to be away from Kashamak for so long but attempts to contact him had proved fruitless and Hassan had been forced to accept that his nonappearance was deliberate.

Was his younger brother hurt that his position as heir apparent might soon be assumed by a newborn baby? Or just angry that Hassan had done what he had vowed he would never do: marry and procreate?

Yet maybe it was better that Kamal wasn't here, demanding to know what his position would be once the baby was born. Leaving Hassan to admit for the first time in his life that he just *didn't know.* That nothing was as it seemed, or as he had thought it would be. That he had been lulled into a curious state of contentment by the sweet nights he now shared with his wife. A false contentment, he reminded himself grimly, and nothing but a pleasurable distraction while they awaited the birth of their child.

Because hadn't there always been the underlying certainty that they would divorce soon afterwards? Hadn't the thought that she might go back to England leaving their baby for him to raise been his secret desire?

But he had come to realise that was never going to happen. Sex taught you much about a woman beyond how she liked you to play with her breasts, and Hassan had discovered a dangerously sweet and soft side to Ella which had defied all his expectations.

Shaking his head to clear his thoughts, he looked at Ella's faintly disgruntled expression. 'What did you say?'

'That I can't carry on doing nothing all day!'

'You are bored?' he questioned.

'Not bored, exactly. More a little restless.' She shrugged her shoulders, aware of the heavy swell of the baby as she moved. 'The gardens are wonderful and so are all the books in the library, but I…'

'What?'

She met his black gaze. What would he say if she told him that she wanted to spend more time with *him*?

Quality time which involved finding out more about him as a person. That seeing him only at breakfast, dinner and when they were in bed at night was proving oddly frustrating. Or maybe the source of her frustration was Hassan's ability to keep her at an emotional distance. She felt as if she could never actually get *through* to him. That after the confidences she'd shared with him during their first night together at the palace, the shutters had come slamming down again. Why did he *do* that? she wondered. Why did he guard his feelings so that she never really knew what was going on in his head?

Oh, he played the part of attentive husband to perfection. He fussed around and made sure she was comfortable, sometimes causing the servants to smile as he positioned a cushion behind her back, like some overzealous nursemaid. Sometimes he even did cute things, like picking her the sweetest pomegranate from the bowl and having the chef prepare it just the way she liked it. And things like that got to her every time.

But somehow it all felt like some sort of displacement therapy. She still felt as if he was pushing her away from him. She fixed him with a steady look. 'I need to get my teeth into something.'

He put the paper down and gave her his undivided attention. 'By doing what, exactly?'

'I want to paint you, Hassan.'

He slanted her a reflective look. 'Run that past me again?'

She took a deep breath, her well-rehearsed words coming out in a rush. 'In London, you promised that I could paint out here if I wanted—and I do. When…

when the baby arrives…' She met his eyes, acutely aware of his sudden watchfulness. 'Well, I certainly won't have time to paint then, will I? So I'd like to do it now, while I can.'

Hassan drummed his fingers against the table, but could see instantly that her idea had merit. His aversion to sitting still was legendary. So wouldn't his people be pleased to have a new portrait of him, as well as giving her something to do?

'I suppose it's a possibility,' he conceded slowly. 'As long as you're aware that my schedule is packed and my time is very precious. I can't sit for hours on end.'

'I know that. I'm not expecting you to. Please, Hassan?' Ella made no attempt to hide her eagerness because she wanted this. She didn't care how snatched their sessions were; she needed to do something other than *wait*. To focus on something other than the baby and her uncertain future, and the sense that her feelings for Hassan were growing stronger than she'd ever intended them to be.

Was that what happened when a man made love to you every night, so beautifully that sometimes it was as much as she could do to prevent tears of joy spilling from her eyes afterwards? Was nature a cunning as well as a random mistress, making a woman form a strong attachment to the man whose child she carried, no matter how emotionally distant that man was?

Well, painters always learned masses about their sitters during portrait sessions—everyone knew that. Maybe this was the only way to get through to him and to find out what really made him tick.

She looked at him enquiringly. 'So can I?'

'How can I possibly deny you when you ask so sweetly?' He picked up his newspaper to resume reading. 'Tell Benedict what it is you need and he'll make sure you get it.'

'I will. And, Hassan?'

'Mmm?'

'Thank you.'

'Just go away and let me read my newspaper, will you?' he growled.

Ella was smiling happily to herself as she went off to find Benedict and, as always, the English aide was surprisingly friendly towards her. Surprising considering he'd delivered the replacement dress and underwear the morning after Alex and Allegra's party. At the time Ella had wondered what he must think of women like her, and how many he had to deal with in the course of a year. Women who fell into bed with a powerful man without really knowing them. Was it strange for Benedict Austin to see that same woman now installed as queen?

But he was nothing if not efficient and had soon allocated her an airy, north-facing room at the far end of the palace, close to the perfumed garden. Deliberately, she left the shutters open so that drifts of sweet scent could waft inside. As a place to paint, it took some beating.

Ella prepared the room thoroughly before the first sitting, intending to make rough sketches in charcoal before attempting to put oil to canvas. She positioned a chair against a completely plain background and decided that she would depict Hassan in his everyday robes. She'd taken the opportunity to study existing portraits in the palace and the few of her husband showed him looking resplendent in his various military uniforms and his more formal sheikh regalia. But she found herself wanting to show the person behind the position, the man not the king. As if by doing that, she might discover more about the man herself.

She sat down to wait for him, realising just how little she really knew about him. He'd still never mentioned his mother, and hadn't said much about his father either. She remembered the day she'd arrived here, when he'd resolutely silenced her questions about his upbringing. And she had let him silence her, determined to maintain a precarious kind of peace no matter what the cost.

But pregnancy was changing more than just her body; it was changing the way she viewed the world. Hassan's mother was not just a person whose name had caused the face of her elder son to darken with pain. She was also a part of the child whose daily kicking inside her belly grew stronger each day. And impending motherhood had also forced Ella to re-examine her views on her own family. She'd recognised that while she might not always approve of the way they behaved, she loved them all very dearly and could never deny their influence on her and the child she carried.

Why, this baby might be a boy who would grow up to be the spitting image of her father! And so what? She let her hand drift to lie on the hard swell of her belly. Was this what her own mother had felt, this powerful bond connecting her to her child? For the first time in her life, she acknowledged how difficult it must have been for her mother to have reared Bobby's children and also the children he'd had with another woman. He'd been unfaithful for much of their marriage and she had simply turned a blind eye to what was going on.

And yet Julie Jackson had somehow managed to keep it together. Ella and her brothers and sisters may not have had much money, but their messy home had been full of laughter, hadn't it? Not like this great, silent palace where Hassan had grown up. She tried to imagine him and his brother playing in the wide corridors and thought how lonely it must have been for them.

'Ella?'

Still lost in her thoughts, she looked up to see that Hassan had arrived at the 'studio,' his dark brows raised in mocking question.

'Sorry.' She smiled at him. 'I was miles away.'

'I can see that for myself. Are you ready for me?'

'Absolutely. Come and sit over here. That's right, just here.'

He sat where she'd asked him to and as she smoothed the headdress which covered his black hair, she resisted the urge to lean over and kiss him. It was one of their rules—or rather, it was one of *his* rules—no physical intimacy outside the bedroom. He'd told her that protocol demanded it, that the aides and ministers who moved with such silent deference around the palace would not approve of their king fooling around with his new bride. Because kisses tended to get out of hand and lead on to other, deeper intimacies. And Ella understood that. Just as she understood that it was yet another way for her husband to keep her at arm's length.

He glanced up at her. 'What must I do?' he asked.

She laughed. 'You know exactly what you must do. You've sat for paintings before.'

'Ah, but it was always with a man, never with the woman who just a few hours ago was lying in my arms.'

'Can you please not talk about sex?' She began to make rapid sweeps on the paper with her stick of charcoal.

'Why not?'

'Because it changes the look on your face. It makes your eyes turn smoky and your mouth grow tense.'

And not just his mouth, Hassan thought wryly, shifting his position slightly. He studied the sweeping movements of her hand and remembered the sketches he'd seen of her sister back in her house in London. The subject matter may have been a little *outré* for his taste, but there was no doubt that she had talent. 'You've never had any formal training?' he questioned.

'Nope.'

'Why not?'

'Because money was too tight to send me to art school.'

'I thought your father made a fortune.'

'He made several fortunes, and then lost them again. Plus, there were his many alimony payments.'

'He is known for his liking of women,' he observed.

'Understatement of the century,' she answered acidly. 'He is also known for his love of grand schemes and the temptation to make a quick buck, which is why there's never been any real money in our family. Everything we owned was only ever temporary.'

His eyes narrowed. 'I see.'

'I wonder if you do,' she said as she put a finger to her lips to indicate that he should stop talking. He'd certainly never known what it was like to worry about paying the gas bill, or to hunt in the cupboard to find nothing but a long-forgotten tin of caviar and to wonder whether slimy fish eggs could possibly fill you up.

For a while she worked in silence and once again Hassan used the opportunity to watch her. Her movements were economical and the studio was completely quiet apart from the scrape of the charcoal and the occasional song of a bird outside. Yet beneath the calm surface of their life, he was aware of a dark kind of uncertainty. A time bomb which was ticking away inexorably. Both of them waiting for something which had the potential to change their lives in ways he couldn't quite imagine. And didn't want to imagine…

He had seen her patting her growing bump, her face growing almost dreamy as she did so. He'd watched her drawing little circles on the tight drum of her belly, as if she was playing some secret game with the child inside her, and his heart had given a painful wrench. He felt jealous, he realised—because his own mother could never have felt a bond like that if she'd been able to just walk away from him and his brother…?

'Hassan, stop frowning.'

'I wasn't.'

'Yes, you were.' She stopped drawing, wondering what had caused that terrible bleakness to enter his eyes. 'What is it, Hassan?' she questioned softly. 'What on earth was making you look that way?'

He saw the understanding on her face and instinct

made him want to push her away. She wanted to probe into his past, as all women did. But with Ella he wasn't in a position to terminate the discussion and then make a cool exit. With Ella there was no escape; the fact that she carried his child had made her a constant in his life. So why not tell her the truth and wipe all that sweet understanding from her face? Why not make her understand where he was coming from, so she'd learn why he could never really love a woman, nor she him?

'I was remembering my mother,' he said.

Something about the silky venom in his voice made the hairs on the back of Ella's neck prickle with apprehension. 'You never talk about her.'

'No. Haven't you ever stopped to wonder why?'

'Of course I have.'

His mouth flattened into a grim line. He'd never told anyone, he realised suddenly. Even he and his brother had never discussed it. They'd locked the memory away in a dark place which was never allowed to see the light of day. As if such a rejection had been too painful to acknowledge, even to themselves. 'Maybe you *should* know, Ella. Maybe it will help explain properly the man that I am.'

Something in his voice was alarming her, and the cold, dark look on his face was scaring her even more.

'Don't tell me if you don't want to,' she whispered, but his face looked so frozen and forbidding that she wondered if he'd actually heard her.

He shook his head as the dark memories bubbled up from the deepest recesses of his mind. 'My mother was a princess from the neighbouring country of Bakamurat,' he said. 'And she was betrothed to my father from an early age—as was the custom at the time. They married when she was just eighteen, and not long after that, I was born. Two years later, Kamal came along.'

'But the marriage wasn't happy?' Ella saw the clenching of his jaw and bit her lip, appalled at her own naivety. 'I'm sorry. That's a stupid question. It can't have been happy if she…left.'

'In those days there was not such a realistic expectation of *happiness* as there is today,' he bit out. 'But, for a while at least, we had a contented family life, the four of us. Or at least, that's how it seemed to me.'

She heard some odd, metallic quality enter his tone. 'But something happened?' she guessed.

'Something most certainly did,' he agreed, his voice bitter. 'My mother went home to visit her sister in Bakamurat, leaving Kamal and me behind. She was gone longer than my father had anticipated, and when she returned, she was…different.'

'How do you mean, *different*?'

For a moment he didn't speak. He had buried this as deeply as he could, but even now he could vividly recall the distracted air which had made it seem as if his mother barely noticed him. The way she'd looked right through him and Kamal as if they hadn't been there. She'd gone off her food, so that the weight had dropped away from her and her beautiful face had seemed to be all large, confused dark eyes. In a way, she had never looked more lovely, and yet even at that early age, Hassan had sensed his father's increasing concern. He remembered the sound of their raised voices when he and Kamal lay in bed at night and the terrible silences at breakfast in the mornings.

'She had fallen in love with a nobleman from Bakamurat.' He heard the distorted sound of his own voice. 'She said she could not live without him. That he was the only man she'd ever loved. My father was as patient as I had ever seen him but eventually his patience wore thin. He told her she must choose between them.'

Ella broke the awful silence with a question she already knew the answer to. 'And she chose *him*?'

'Yes. She chose her lover over her husband and she left behind her two little boys while she went off to find what she described as the only man who had ever really understood her.'

'Who told you that?'

'My father.'

Ella nodded, her heart going out to him, cursing the loose tongues of broken-hearted adults. 'Sometimes parents tell their children too much,' she said falteringly. 'I remember my own mother sobbing and telling me things about my father I wish she hadn't said. I think she forgot who was the parent and who was the child. Sometimes people act inappropriately when their emotions get the better of them.'

'Exactly! Which is why I don't *do* emotion—or "love."' His lips curved into a cynical half-smile, thinking that she couldn't have given him a better platform for the truth if she'd tried. 'Why embrace something which makes people act shamefully?' he demanded. 'Which eats into what is good and what is true. And it changes—that's the truth of it. Love is as inconstant as the wind. My mother vowed to spend her life with my father and she broke that vow. So how can anyone ever put their trust in it?'

Ella put the charcoal down, afraid that he would see the sudden trembling of her fingers. The warning in his voice was implicit; she heard it loud and clear. But she wanted to know the ending. Whether any happiness had been squeezed from the sour story he was telling her.

'What happened to your mother?' she questioned softly.

He shook his head, because the supposed retribution which had been heaped upon the woman who had given birth to him had brought him no comfort. 'The shame of her desertion went with her. Her nobleman would not marry a woman who was tainted in such a way. I don't think he'd ever intended to marry her in the first place. She'd just built up the fantasy in her head. And of course, my father refused to take her back.'

'Did she want to come back?' breathed Ella.

'Oh, yes. It seemed that she realised just what she had lost—two little children and a man who loved her. But it was too late and his pride would not countenance it. He had been made a fool of once and would not risk it happening again. She began to neglect herself. She wasn't eating properly. She went to Switzerland and it was there, in the cold of the winter snows, that she caught pneumonia.'

Ella didn't need to hear the words to know that his mother had died; she could read it from the bleak look on his face. 'And you never...you never saw her again?'

'No.'

'Hassan—'

'No!' he said again, shaking away the soft hand which had reached out towards him. Standing, he moved away from the chair and her tantalising proximity.

But Ella went after him because the look of bleakness on his ravaged face was more than she could bear. She moved up to his tensed, hunched body and, rising up on tiptoes, she put her arms around him.

'Hassan,' she breathed into his ear. 'Darling, darling Hassan.'

His heart was thumping and he could feel the contrasting softness of her cheek against his. He should have pushed her away, but how could he do that when the hard curve of her baby bump was pressing against him and her welcoming arms were enfolding him. And that was the moment that his long-suppressed emotions ruptured. When anger and hurt and shame and resentment all came swimming darkly to the surface and threatened to swamp him.

He opened his mouth to groan but her lips were reaching towards his and somehow he was kissing her, kissing her with an urgent kind of hunger he'd never felt before. His hands splayed over her breasts and her muffled little cries urged him on, and as he felt the nipples harden beneath his palms, a primitive hunger began to rise in him.

With a low moan like the sound of a wounded animal, he pulled away from her before locking the door and, when he turned back, Ella could see from the look of dark intent on his face just what he was going to do.

His embrace was hard and his lips heated, but she matched him kiss for kiss. Greedily, she scrabbled at the silk of his robes as he slithered hers up over her thighs, his fingers skating over the cool skin there until he found the molten heat which awaited him.

She did not dare cry out, not even when he thrust deep inside her, taking her from behind because it was more comfortable that way, before beginning his inexorable rhythm. Ella swallowed as he caught hold of her shoulders, his lips on her hair as he whispered to her, strange, fractured words in his native tongue. It had never felt quite like this: with all her senses heightened by the emotion of what he'd told her and the fact that Hassan was breaking his own rules by making love to her in the makeshift studio.

Her orgasm happened quickly—almost too quickly, it seemed—and it was as if she had given him everything she had to give. She felt his own, final thrust. Heard the little choking sound he made as he clung to her, spilling his seed deep inside her.

'Hassan,' she whispered.

For a moment he couldn't speak as he sucked in gulps of air, sanity returning to cool his ardour like a summer rainstorm. Against the rumpled spill of her hair, Hassan briefly closed his eyes, a wave of guilt washing over him as he realised just what he had done. He had used her, as he used all women. He had taken the sweet comfort she was offering him and had turned it into the only commodity he was familiar with. Sex.

'That should never have happened,' he said hoarsely.

'But I'm *glad* it happened!' came her fierce reply.

Biting back his remorse, he withdrew from her, adjusting himself before turning her around to cup her face in his hands. 'So now do you understand why I am the man I am?' he demanded. 'Why I can't love. Do you understand that, Ella?'

She looked at him, her heart twisting with pain, wanting to tell him that his mother's rejection didn't mean that *all* women were going to do the same. That she would love him and cherish him if only he would give her the chance.

'I understand perfectly,' she said softly. 'But these things aren't set in stone, Hassan. There's no reason why you can't change.' *I can help you change.*

He saw the hope and understanding written on her face and a bitter wave of recrimination washed over him. She didn't have a clue, did she? How horrified she would be if she knew how ruthless he had been. If she discovered that he'd brought her out here hoping that she would leave him. And leave their baby too.

He shook his head as he unlocked the door and wrenched it open. 'I think we'd better call it a day. This session is over and I have work to do.'

And he swept from the room. Just like that. Leaving Ella watching him, blinking away the sudden shimmer of tears which had sprung to her eyes.

She glanced down at the start she'd made on the drawing which now bore the outline of Hassan's face. But it was strange how a few black lines had somehow managed to capture a true likeness of the man she had married. The hawk-like nose and the shadowed jut of his jaw. The autocratic cheekbones and the empty black eyes.

A proud man who had told her he could never love.

Closing the door quietly behind her, Ella left the studio and walked in silence along the scented marble corridor towards her suite.

CHAPTER TWELVE

SO THIS was how it was going to be. Everything had changed, yet nothing had changed, and Ella felt as if she was living in a strange kind of limbo. She moved around the beautiful palace feeling like a gatecrasher who the benign host had allowed to remain at the party.

The stupid thing was that, at first, Hassan's emotional outpouring had given her hope. She'd thought that once he'd given himself time to reflect on her words that he might come around to her way of thinking. To realise that change *was* possible. That anything was possible if you wanted it enough.

And maybe the simple truth of it was that he just didn't want it. Maybe the thought of allowing himself to *feel* stuff secretly repulsed him. That his childhood experiences had scarred him too deeply for him ever to contemplate living his life in a different way.

Because he behaved as if nothing had happened. As if he hadn't torn open the blackness which seemed to envelop his heart and allowed her to glimpse the bitter pain which lay beneath.

Once again, the barriers came crashing down, only this time it was worse than before. Because now she had something with which to compare it. She'd felt a snatch of real closeness when he'd opened up to her about his past. When she'd felt as though they'd discovered a new honesty…and when she'd realised how easy it would be to love this proud and tortured man.

But that was all now a distant memory; the hot passion which had flared between them now mocked her, because Hassan had told her that sex was no longer on the agenda.

Her hands had trembled when he'd dropped *that* particular bombshell. 'You're saying that you no longer find me attractive?'

He had shaken his head, still not quite believing that he had opened up to her. Still dazed by the powerful and very basic sex which had followed, which had left him feeling…what? As if she'd laid him bare on every level. As if she could see right into his soul. 'I'm saying that your pregnancy is getting too advanced,' he responded. 'And I don't think sex is a good idea.'

Ella had turned away to hide her distress. And so the pleasure she'd found in his arms became nothing but a taunting series of memories. The nights were nothing but long, lonely hours to be endured. Her enormous bed allowed them both to lie there without touching, and the longer this went on, the more impossible it became to return to what they'd had before.

Ella would hold her breath as she felt the mattress dip beneath Hassan's weight, and perhaps if she hadn't been so pregnant, she might have attempted some form of seduction. As it was, even sitting up was a big, lumbering effort. She didn't even want to think of how clumsy it would look if she tried to launch herself at him. Anyway, such plans were pretty pointless since

Hassan would fall asleep almost as soon as his head touched the pillow, while she was left staring at the moon shadows flickering over the ceiling.

One morning she awoke to find him leaning over her, his dark face creased with concern, and for one crazy moment, she thought he was going to kiss her. Her lips parted as eagerly as a young chick on the nest, but his face became shuttered as he drew back from her.

'You look exhausted,' he observed quietly. 'Can't you sleep?'

'No.' She waited for him to ask him why and wondered if she dared tell him the reason. *Because I miss you. I miss you touching me. Kissing me. Making love to me. Because I'm scared of the future...and I'm only just beginning to realise the heartache which lies ahead if we're living these separate lives.* But she wasn't going to beg. Or whine. She hadn't quite sunk to *that.* She kept her voice light. 'Nobody ever died from lack of sleep.'

'No, but it isn't fair to you or the baby to see you looking so exhausted,' he said harshly. 'I will move back into my own rooms and sleep there from now on.'

Her eyes beseeched him to reconsider even if her pride stopped her from asking him outright, but he was true to his word. It didn't take long for one of his valets to move his few possessions out of her suite, and after that night, Ella slept alone.

As the days passed, so her loneliness increased. With her sickness firmly in the past and without the diversion of long and erotic nights with Hassan, Ella's life in the palace seemed empty and pointless. Only continuing with her husband's portrait, into which she poured all her thwarted passion and despair, helped fill the long, waiting days.

But that was her only distraction. The constant heat and lack of seasonal change were having a disorientating effect on her. She felt like someone who had awoken from a long sleep and found themselves in an unknown place. The flowers in the garden looked fake; the sky seemed too blue to be real. The beautiful, gilded palace began to feel like a glittering cage.

Hard to believe that it was early December and, back home, everyone would be gearing up to Christmas. She thought about the glittering lights which twinkled along Regent Street and the supermarkets which would be stuffed to the gills with chocolate. She thought about those tacky paper chains her father used to insist on, because no matter what his faults were, he absolutely loved Christmas and had passed on that love to his children.

And crazily, she began to miss her family. *All* her family. Her mother might be a walkover where her father was concerned, but she had always been there when you needed her. The email correspondence they'd been sharing suddenly seemed woefully inadequate, especially the last one which had expressed a wistful desire to 'see my little girl looking pregnant.'

She even missed her sisters. She hadn't had a chance to talk to Allegra about her engagement. And while Izzy might be erratic at times, she was filled with an energy and enthusiasm which Ella missed.

Now that all the Jacksons knew she was pregnant, would there really be any shame in admitting defeat and going home and accepting help from her family instead of from Hassan? Because his help came with a price tag which was beginning to seem way too high. She didn't *have* to be some sort of passive wimp who just took whatever type of behaviour the sheikh doled out to her.

Her troubled thoughts wouldn't leave her and eventually it dawned on her that she wanted to go home. And that she would have to tell Hassan. She would emphasise that her trip out here hadn't been wasted because at least it had enabled them to get to know each other and to establish a degree of civility. And she wouldn't be unreasonable over access either. In fact, she would make sure that he had as much of it as he liked. Because she would never allow a man who had been neglected by his mother to be kept at a distance by his son or daughter.

Once she had psyched herself up enough, she sat down to breakfast, her manner curiously calm as she took her place opposite her husband.

She went through the ritual of drizzling honey onto her bowl of yoghurt. She could sense him watching her, so suddenly she put her spoon down and looked up to meet the dark fire of his eyes.

'You're still not sleeping?' he questioned before she could say a word. 'Even though you now have the bed to yourself?'

'No.' She shook her head. 'It's getting much too uncomfortable to sleep.'

'Is there anything I can do?' he questioned.

For a moment she was tempted to say yes. To tell him to come back to her bed and get close to her. And despite her determination not to, she allowed herself a brief glimpse of how it *could* have been. She imagined a scenario where joys and problems could have been discussed, and shared. And then she thought about what it *was*: an empty relationship with a man who was cold and unloving towards her. Who had told her emphatically that he *couldn't* love. What woman in her right mind would settle for something like that?

'Yes.' She hesitated, clasping her fingers together just in case they started trembling. 'Actually, there is.'

Something in the tone of her voice made his eyes narrow. 'And what might that be, Ella?'

There was a pause. 'I want to go home.'

Hassan nodded as a terrible tearing sense of inevitability twisted his gut. 'Home?' he questioned.

'Yes, home. I want to see my family.'

'But I thought your family drove you mad?'

'And they do—frequently!' Her gaze was very steady as she looked at him. 'But at least they *feel* stuff. At least their hearts are in the right place, even if they often get it wrong!'

Her implication was crystal clear and suddenly Hassan was forced to accept what he would have once considered impossible. That, for all their faults, at least the Jacksons had the courage to face up to their own emotions. Their lives might be chaotic at times, but they didn't run away and hide from their feelings. And yet didn't he despise that kind of messy emotion? Surely that wasn't a brief pang of *envy* he was experiencing? His mouth hardened. 'And you miss them?'

'I do.' She nodded, steeling her heart. 'I feel like a shadow here, Hassan. As if I'm invisible. I want to fly home so that I can see a few friendly and familiar faces and eat some mince pies and listen to c-c-carols….'

To her horror, she realised that tears had sprung to her eyes and when Hassan made to move towards her she waved him away. 'D-don't!' she stumbled, knowing that if he touched her she would be lost. 'Please don't. You've made it very clear you don't want me near you, so please don't let a few tears tempt you from your chosen path. My life has telescoped down to this beautiful place which now feels like a prison, though I'm starting to wonder if that's how you wanted it to be all along.'

Hassan sucked in a breath. He felt as if he had wandered into a maze of his own making, where darkness had suddenly fallen. He had pushed her away in order to protect himself. Pushed her and pushed her until she had decided that she could take no more. Now she wanted out, and he had no one to blame but himself. He looked at her pale face, at the swollen curve of her belly, and was overcome with a terrible wave of regret.

'But you're nearly thirty-six weeks pregnant,' he pointed out.

'So?'

'So the airlines won't allow you to fly.'

'You've got your own plane, Hassan, so I can't see *that* will be a problem.'

In silence, he got up from the table and walked over to the window, his mind teeming with conflicting thoughts. What if he asked her to stay, what then? What did she really want from him? he wondered. Deep in his heart he knew. She wanted the *impossible*!

She wanted the man he could never be, the close and loving partner all women were programmed to want.

He turned away from the window to see her looking at him, her blue eyes wary, her arms folded defensively across her breasts. And suddenly he realised that this was the one area of his life where he had consistently shown a complete lack of courage. Was he so afraid of reliving the pain of his childhood that he wouldn't take any risks for a chance of happiness? Couldn't he at least *try* to be what she wanted?

'Maybe you're right,' he said slowly. 'I *have* been guilty of neglecting you. But if it's any consolation, I thought I was doing it for the best.'

'For the best for who? For you? Or for me?' she shot back. 'And meanwhile, you mooch around being all king-like and solitary, while I've been cooped up inside this wretched palace for weeks!'

'I realise that.' He drew a breath, unused to this new-found role of mediator in his own marriage. 'Which is why I wondered if you'd like to go on a trip?'

'That's what I'm proposing, Hassan—a trip back home to England.'

'No, not that.' He shook his head. 'My brother has a traditional Bedouin tent situated on the edge of the Serhetabat Desert. It's not far from here, although it feels like a different world. We could go and stay there for a couple of nights.' His black eyes narrowed. 'It would give you a break. Give you a complete change of scenery. Wouldn't you like that, Ella?'

Despite all that had happened between them, Ella felt tempted. Surely two nights in a Bedouin tent meant that they'd connect again—and wasn't that something she still wanted even though her aching heart told her that she was crazy to want it? She wondered what his offer represented. Whether it was his way of saying that he understood her frustrations and wanted to make some amends. Or whether it was simply a sweetener to get her to do what he wanted and stay in Kashamak.

'I don't know,' she prevaricated.

Her reluctance didn't surprise him and neither did the fierce light which sparked from her blue eyes. Hassan realised that he *admired* her defiance and her determination to stand up to him. All the things which he'd once claimed not to like in a woman, he found amazingly attractive in Ella. And yet didn't nature ensure that what attracted also repelled? Didn't what drew him to her also drive him away, with a feeling which was the closest he'd known to fear?

'It is a very beautiful place,' he said steadily. 'Which you really ought to see for yourself. The desert sky when it's washed in moonlight is a sight not to be missed.'

'And afterwards, Hassan? What then?'

He felt an aching dryness in his throat as he met the question in her eyes and knew he couldn't offer her empty promises. He could take this first step and see where it led, but he wasn't in the habit of dishing out false hope. 'If you decide that you're missing England so much, then of course you must go back. I won't stop you, and I will support you and our child in whatever way I can.'

Her heart pounding, Ella stared at him. He was offering her freedom, and never had an offer seemed like such a poisoned chalice. 'And you wouldn't mind?'

He shrugged. 'Naturally, it would be easier to keep you and the baby here,' he said heavily. 'But I don't intend to force you to stay. Ultimately, it has to be your decision.'

Ella shook her head in frustration. With his burnished skin and magnificent body, he might look like every woman's fantasy come to life, but inside he was frozen. *Frozen.* It was like dealing with some sort of robot, one who was conditioned to move but never to feel! *He doesn't care whether you go or stay! Nothing has changed in all the weeks you've been here.*

The voice inside her head mocked her hesitation and yet something inside her made her want this trip. Some illogical little hope which refused to die, despite all the odds which were stacked up against it.

'Then let's go,' she said as she stared into his black eyes. 'Maybe seeing the desert sky washed with moonlight is exactly what I need.'

CHAPTER THIRTEEN

THEY left the next morning in a four-wheel drive which Hassan drove himself, the powerful car eating up the miles of straight, desert roads. Ella was determined to make the most of what might be her one and only desert trip, but her excitement was tempered by the niggling backache she'd developed during the night and which seemed to be preventing her from getting comfortable.

She felt *edgy.* Wondering why was she was going to the bother of putting herself through all this—the newlywed queen being shown the desert by her sheikh king—when it was nothing but a sham. Hassan had probably only offered to take her in order to placate her. To keep the little lady quiet. Restlessly, she wriggled in her seat.

Hassan shot her a glance as he saw her tug impatiently at the seat belt which was straining over her swollen belly. 'Are you okay?'

'I'm absolutely fine,' she said. 'So will you please keep your eyes off me and look at the road instead?'

She had been in an irritable mood all morning, he acknowledged, but he did as she asked, silence falling as they drove along until he saw a familiar marking on the horizon.

'Look,' he said. 'Straight ahead and a little to the left. Can you see it?'

Ella screwed up her eyes to see a small blot on the stark landscape. As they grew closer, she could see that it was a tent, but nothing like as glamorous as she'd been expecting. Apart from its dense, black colour, it just seemed like a much bigger version of the tents you saw at music festivals.

'Does it stand empty all the time?' she asked.

'This one does. Kamal uses it only infrequently. I sent some servants here earlier to make it habitable for us, but they will have returned to the palace by now.'

He stopped the car in a spray of sand and went round to the passenger door. The pure, clean air filled his lungs as he inhaled deeply and he looked up into the deep cobalt of the sky before helping his wife down. It had been a long time since he'd been in the desert for the purpose of pleasure, rather than war, and inevitably he felt the fizz of exhilaration. Stealing a glance at Ella's face, he helped her down from the car. Maybe not quite pleasure, he amended wryly—at least, not for her. Endurance might be a more accurate description, judging by her expression.

'Welcome,' he said. 'To a genuine Bedouin tent. For the weary traveller, the sight of one of these is like stumbling across an oasis.'

Ella dredged up a smile from somewhere. She was feeling very weary herself, and it was much hotter out here than she'd imagined. But she recognised that Hassan was trying hard to please her, so shouldn't she just try to enjoy the experience? Fanning her hand across her face, she made her way over to the entrance of the tent, but as she pulled back the flap and stepped inside the surprisingly cool interior, she sucked in a breath of amazement.

Lit by intricate metal lamps, the canopied ceiling was hung with rich fabrics of scarlet and bronze, all shot with shimmering gold. Rose and turquoise wall hangings glimmered with a soft intensity, and on the woven rugs stood low sofas, cushions and bronze tables. The air was scented with something spicy and evocative and for a moment Ella's niggling backache was forgotten.

'Oh, wow,' she said softly, because it was exactly like stepping into an illustration from the *Arabian Nights*. 'It's beautiful.'

But Hassan's attention wasn't on the decor. He was momentarily transfixed by the look on his wife's face. By the parting of her rose-petal lips and the widening of her ice-blue eyes. *She* was beautiful, he thought suddenly. Her face bare of makeup and her body swollen with his child, he thought he'd never seen anyone look quite so lovely in his life. *And she wants to leave you. She wants to leave you, and you have no one to blame but yourself.*

'Shall we sit down?' he questioned unsteadily. 'And I'll make you some of the tea for which the Bedouin are famous.'

A wave of dizziness swept over her as Ella nodded, cumbersomely lowering herself onto one of the cushions. 'If you like,' she said.

He set about boiling water and measuring out herbs

and sugar before adding them to the heavy pot in which the tea was made. But he turned round when he heard the ragged little sigh she made and saw her eyes momentarily close.

'Are you okay?'

Her lids flew open again. 'I would be if you'd just stop fussing!' She sounded as if she was spoiling for a fight but Hassan didn't react. She's just emotional, he told himself. And she has every right to be. He carried over a tray bearing tiny cups and the steaming tea.

'What's that funny smell?' she questioned suspiciously.

'It's probably the habak and marmaraya. They're the desert herbs which gives the tea its distinct flavour. The habak tastes a little like mint.'

Ella swallowed. 'I think I'm going to be sick.'

'It isn't *that* bad.'

But his attempt at humour was forgotten as Ella suddenly realised that something momentous was happening to her.

'Hassan, I feel weird.'

'What kind of weird?'

She swallowed. 'I think I'm going to have the baby.'

'Don't be silly.'

'Don't you dare tell me I'm silly!' she flared back. 'How the hell would you know? You've suddenly gained a qualification in obstetrics, have you?'

'You've got another four weeks to go.'

'I know exactly how long I've got to go and I don't *care*! This baby's coming *now*!' Staggering to her feet, she felt the unexpected warm rush of liquid cascading down her leg and she stared down in numb horror as realisation began to dawn on her. 'Hassan!' she gasped, raising her head to meet the disbelief in his eyes. 'My waters have just broken!'

Hassan froze. He thought of the clean, bright interior of the labour ward at the hospital in Samaltyn, of the fully trained teams of doctors and nurses who could be summoned at a moment's notice, and denial washed over him. 'They can't have done!'

'They have! Look! *Look!*' Reaching out, she caught hold of his hand, her nails digging roughly into his flesh. 'Hassan, that was a definitely a contraction!'

'Are you sure?'

'Of course I'm sure! Oh, heavens! The baby's coming and we're stuck out in the middle of the bloody desert!'

One glance at her was enough to convince him that she was speaking the truth and his instinct was to panic like never before. Desperately, his thoughts whirled as he thought about the options which lay open to them. Was there time to get her back to Samaltyn? He heard her gasp and clutch at her stomach with her free hand and he knew there was not. Sweet flower of the desert, why ever had he brought her out here at such a time?

But her blue eyes were dark with fear and Hassan knew he had to quash his own spiralling terror and get a grip. He had to be there for her. He had let her down so many ways in the past but this time she was relying on him like never before.

Carefully, he laid her back down on the cushions, barely noticing the nails which were digging into his hands so hard he could feel them drawing blood. His heart was pounding frantically as he leaned over her and squeezed her hand. 'Stay here!' he commanded.

'What else do you think I'm going to do?' She clung onto his hand as she felt him pulling away. 'Hassan! Where are you going?'

He cursed as he stared down at the flat line on his cellphone. 'I'll have to go outside, to ring the hospital. There's no damned signal in here!'

'Don't leave me!' she whispered.

'Sweetheart. I'll be right back.'

Ella felt as if this was all happening to someone else and the unfamiliar *sweetheart* only compounded it. As if the woman lying back against a pile of cushions, gasping with pain, was someone she'd once met but didn't really know. Dimly, she could hear Hassan outside the tent barking out a series of instructions in his native tongue. Hurry up, she thought faintly. Just hurry *up*!

She had never been so glad to see anyone as when he came running back into the tent and crouched down beside her. But then another contraction rocked right through her and she clung to him, panting for breath.

'It's okay,' he said, closing his eyes briefly against her damp hair as he held her. 'The hospital is sending a helicopter with a full obstetric crew on board. They say that you've probably got plenty of time before you deliver, especially as this is a first baby.'

She shook her head as another contraction racked through her body, feeling as if someone had sent a red-hot poker slicing up inside her. 'No!' she croaked.

Helplessly, his gaze raked over her ashen face. No,

what? 'Just hang on in there,' he urged from between gritted teeth. 'They'll be here soon.'

'Hassan,' she gasped, sweat breaking out on her brow as another contraction came. Her nails dug into him even more. 'They're wrong.'

'Who is?'

'The hospital. I—' She gasped as the pain made speech momentarily impossible. 'I think this baby's coming now!'

His heart pounded. 'It can't be.'

'Yes, it *can*.'

'How can you be sure?'

'I just *am*!'

Desperately, he looked out into the starkness of the empty desert which could be seen through the flaps of the tent. How long would the helicopter take, he wondered distractedly, and would it be able to pinpoint their position? 'I'll go outside and get a signal. Speak to the doctor—'

'Hassan, there isn't time!' She gripped even tighter as another contraction tightened its vice-like grip around her. 'Just stay!' she gasped. 'Hassan, I need you here with me. I need *you*. Please.'

He saw the change in her and realised that she was speaking the truth. That their baby was about to be born. Here. Now. And that he was the only person who could help her. He was going to have to deliver the baby. *His* baby.

He felt a brief roaring in his ears before his head cleared and he suddenly became calm. It was like being in battle, when the sounds of melee all around him suddenly blurred into silence and he could see nothing but the task which lay ahead.

'I'm here,' he said softly, injecting calm into his voice as he began to loosen her clothing. 'I'm here for you and everything is going to be fine. Shh, Ella. Just take it easy. Breathe very slowly. That's right. Very slowly. Nature knows what to do.'

She looked up at him. 'I'm scared.'

So was he—more scared than he'd ever been. But Hassan had had a lifetime of experience in hiding the way he felt. Right now, he'd never been so glad of that. Gripping her hands tightly, he looked deep into her eyes. 'Trust me, Ella,' he said softly. 'I am here for you, and believe me when I tell you that it's going to be okay.'

Ella nodded and, despite the pain and fear, her trust in him at that moment was total and complete.

He found a soft blanket, remembering the first time he'd seen a foal being born and recalling what the stable boy had told him: that mares were like humans, that every birth was different and that most of what happened did so without the need for intervention. Please let that be the case this time, he prayed silently as he brushed her sweat-soaked hair away from her face.

'Hassan!'

'I'm here. Keep breathing. Go on, breathe.'

The vice-like contractions were increasing in frequency and intensity. She began to anticipate the next one, wondering if it could possibly be as bad as the one before, only to discover that it was worse. Was this what every woman who'd ever given birth had experienced?

'I can't bear it!' she cried.

'Yes, you can. You can, Ella. You can do anything you want to do because you're strong. The strongest woman I ever met.'

At any other time such words would have moved her but now they were nudged onto the periphery of her mind as another great contraction racked through her. Ella bit hard down on her lip as something in her body changed and she looked up into Hassan's black eyes, saw the question written in them and realised that something very powerful was happening. 'I think the baby's coming right now,' she gritted out. 'Oh, Hassan! Hassan, please help me!'

He moved just in time to see the slick crown of a head appear. 'You're doing fine,' he said unsteadily. 'You're amazing. You're nearly there.'

Dimly she remembered what she'd been taught: not to push until the need to push was unbearable. Guided by that and governed by an instinct as old as time itself, she held on to that thought. 'Yes,' she breathed, her face contorted with effort. 'Yes.'

He heard the keening sound she made and his heart began to race. Every sense intensified, he moved as if he was on some sort of autopilot. 'That's perfect,' he said roughly. Suddenly, he was aware that he was looking down at the baby's matted black hair and a great lump rose in his throat. 'Just one more push, Ella. Do you think you can do that?'

'Yes! No! I don't know!'

'Yes, you can. Ella, you can.'

The moan she made sounded as if it had been torn from some unimaginably deep place inside her and

Hassan stretched out his palms to form a miniature cradle just as his baby was born into them.

His baby.

He felt the slippery unfamiliarity of new life in his hands and his heart clenched with terror as nothing else happened. The whole world seemed suspended in that moment of absolute silence before a lusty cry split the air.

His eyes blurred with tears and he looked down to see the wriggling form of a tiny yet perfect human being in his hands, which he quickly wrapped in the soft blanket before laying the child gently on Ella's stomach.

Her voice seemed to come from a long way off. 'Is…is everything okay?'

'She's perfect, my darling. Perfect. Just like you.'

Ella's hand was trembling as she reached out to touch her baby, amazement and relief compounded by the realisation that Hassan was crying. And that he had been there for her.

He had been there for her when she most needed him. On every level he had delivered. He *could* be the man she wanted him to be: emotional and strong and equal.

She gave a ragged breath as she heard helicopter propellers descending from out of the desert sky, and even while she was glad that help was arriving, she wanted to hold on to that private moment for ever. Just the three of them in their own little world. With none of the fears that once they stepped outside that tent, Hassan would go back to being the cool and distant man of the past.

CHAPTER FOURTEEN

HASSAN shut the door of the studio behind him and began to walk down the wide marble corridor towards the nursery suite. His heart was heavy but he knew he could not put off this moment any longer. It was time to accept and face up to the truth.

He'd been waiting for the right moment. For Ella to properly recover from the birth. For the doctors to give both mother and daughter the thumbs-up. And for this terrible sense of remorse to leave him.

Yet it wouldn't leave him. It clung to him like glue. Deep down he knew there was only one thing which would make him feel better—ironically, the very thing which would bring his world crashing down about him.

He found Ella standing by the window in the main salon, looking out onto one of the smaller fountains where a plume of water formed a graceful curve. Barefooted beneath her cream silk robe, her hair was hanging loose down her back and she turned round when she heard him enter. Her blue eyes were as bright as usual but he saw darkness in their depths, as if she, too, had recognised that the moment of truth was here.

'Your father has been on the phone,' he said heavily.

'Oh? What did he say?'

He saw the faint lines crisscrossing her pale brow and realised that she must have lived much of her life like this. On a kind of knife edge, never knowing what her father was going to do or say next. His mouth hardened. And hadn't it been exactly the same when she'd met him? Hadn't he brought that same element of uncertainty into her life? He wondered why he had never seen that before, but the answer came to him almost immediately. He'd never seen it because he'd never allowed himself to see it.

'He wants to know whether we are planning to go to Alex and Allegra's wedding.'

She looked at him. 'And what did you tell him?'

'I said that we hadn't decided. Because that's the truth of it, isn't it, Ella? We haven't decided so many things, and I don't think attending your sister's wedding is top of the list of things we need to resolve.'

Ella nodded, but his words made her heart plummet. She knew they couldn't keep putting off the inevitable, yet she was afraid to face up to it. Afraid of what lay ahead—of a cold and empty future without her husband by her side.

Hadn't she hoped that they could just forget the past and move on? Capitalise on the love—yes, love—which had pulsed through the air between them after their baby had been born. That moment of pure and unfettered joy when their eyes had met and they had silently acknowledged the new life they had created.

She looked at Hassan now, wondering whether they should postpone any decisions for a few days longer. He still looked slightly shell-shocked, even though it had been a week since they had returned from the desert. The longest seven days of her life, and easily the most eventful.

They'd been dazed and disorientated as they had entered the celebrating city of Samaltyn, cradling their newborn daughter with pride. They'd called her Rihana because they both liked the name, and when Ella had discovered it meant 'sweet herb,' that had clinched it. Because hadn't Hassan been making sweet, herbal tea when she'd gone into labour? For a while she'd been on such a high of hormones and emotion that it was all too easy to pretend they were like any normal couple who'd just had a baby.

But now the intensely intimate memories of the birth had started to fade, leaving a couple who had resolved nothing. Who had begun to eye each other warily, as if each waiting for the other to make a move. She found herself wishing that she was back in that simple Bedouin tent again, where she had felt so incredibly close to Hassan. But she couldn't keep getting herself into medical emergencies just to get him to show some *feelings*, could she?

'You said you wanted to go home,' Hassan said roughly, his words breaking into her thoughts and sounding almost like an accusation. 'Have you thought any more about that?'

Ella winced as his stark words brought reality crashing in. During the ecstatic days following Rihana's birth, it had been all too easy to forget about her insecurities, but Hassan's question brought it into such sharp focus that she could no longer ignore it. Her insecurity was all bound up in her marriage, she realised, in her relationship with him. And nothing had changed.

Yes, during those heightened and unbelievable moments in the desert, she'd felt as close to him as she'd imagined it was possible for a man and woman to feel. When the helicopter had landed and the obstetricians had rushed in and taken over, before leaving the two—no, three—of them alone again for a few minutes, it had seemed a very precious time indeed.

Their eyes had met over the dark head of the baby who had latched so eagerly onto her breast and she thought she'd read something other than dazed pride in Hassan's expression. She'd clung to the hope that he might now want to forge a new and closer future. A future for *all* of them.

But all those hopes had evaporated by the time they returned to the palace, where it seemed that normal procedure was to be renewed almost immediately. Hassan had done what he did best and occupied himself with the practicalities. Making sure that she had the best after-care. Issuing statements to the world media and declining to the give them the full and dramatic story of Rihana's birth. Filling the nursery with a department-store quota of soft, fluffy toys.

Yet the subsequently smooth transition from pregnant queen to new mother seemed to have left Ella feeling just as displaced as before. *And nothing would ever change so long as she was with Hassan,* she realised. Why would it, when he didn't seem to want anything more than this?

Now she focused on his words and realised that it

was worse than she'd thought. That he actively *wanted* her to go.

'I'd thought I'd wait—'

'For what, Ella?' he interrupted bitterly. 'For me to bond even more with Rihana so that I'll find it unbearable when you take her away from me?'

'You want me to go,' she stated dully.

Hassan flinched. Was she determined to twist the knife, to make this even more painful than it already was? And could he really blame her, if that was the case, for surely he deserved everything she chose to heap upon his head?

'I can't see any alternative.' His voice was harsh. 'Surely you can't wait to get away from a man who forced you to come here even though you wanted to stay in London. A man who doesn't have a heart, nor any compassion. Because I now have looked at myself through your eyes, Ella, and I do not like what I see.'

'What on earth are you talking about?' she whispered.

He shook his head as the memory swam into his mind, like dark, distorting smoke. 'That portrait!' he grated. 'I have just been into the studio and seen the man that you have painted. A ravaged man—'

'Hassan—'

'Isn't there some novel where the man agrees a trade-off with the devil for eternal youth?' he demanded. 'And meanwhile there's a portrait in the attic which shows the growing darkness inside him?'

'It's called *The Picture of Dorian Gray*,' she said automatically.

'Well, the darkness is right there on that canvas

you've done of me, only I haven't even had the eternal youth in exchange,' he said bitterly, until he realised that wasn't quite true. Because in a way, every man who ever had a child was given the gift of eternal youth. Only he would never see the daily miracle of his daughter's developing life. He would be resigned to meeting her on high days and holidays, their precious time eaten into by the initial adjustment of having to reacquaint themselves every time they met. He would grow older never really knowing his child, and he would have no one to blame but himself.

Ella stared at him. 'What are you trying to say, Hassan?'

He knew that he had to tell her. Everything. Every damned thing. She had to know the terrible lengths to which he had been prepared to go—and that would be the end of their marriage, once and for all.

'Do you want to know the real reason why I was so insistent you came out to Kashamak when I discovered you were pregnant?' he demanded.

She remembered the way he had expressed it at the time—as concern for her morning sickness and the need for someone to look after her. But she hadn't been naive enough to think they were the real reasons. 'It was about control, wasn't it? About making sure that I conducted the pregnancy in a way you approved of.'

'Yes, it was. But deep down, it was even more manipulative than that,' he said quietly. 'I thought you'd have trouble adjusting, you see. That motherhood would cramp your style.'

'Cramp my style?' she repeated blankly.

'That was when I was still labouring under the illusion that you were a good-time girl. A social butterfly. I thought you'd hate your life here and you'd want to be free again. And that's what I wanted too.'

Ella saw the muscle which was working frantically at his cheek and the expression in his black eyes. But for once, they were not empty. Instead they were filled with the most terrible look of *bleakness* she had ever seen. Even worse than the time he'd told her about his mother.

'You wanted me to leave?' she guessed slowly. 'And to leave the baby behind, with you?'

He winced, but he did not look away from her. The truth was painful but he could not deny it—and didn't he deserve this pain? Didn't he deserve all the recriminations she chose to hurl at his head? 'Yes.'

'To bring her up as your father once did, without a mother?'

'Yes.' He shook his head, as if he was coming out of a deep sleep. 'It's only been during the past few weeks that I realised I couldn't possibly go through with it. That I couldn't inflict on my own child what I had suffered myself. But for a while, the intention was there.' He met the question which blazed from her eyes. 'How you must hate me, Ella.'

For a second she thought that perhaps it would be easier if she did, because the man who stood before her was the most complex individual she'd ever met. And didn't she suspect that the dark and complicated side of him *wanted* her to hate him? That it would be easier for him if she did, if she pushed him away and thus reinforced all his prejudices against women.

But Ella realised that nobody had ever been there

for Hassan, not emotionally. After his mother had left, he'd never let anyone get close enough to try, and she wondered if she had the courage to do that. To risk being rejected by him all over again.

Yet what choice did she have? To live a life blighted by regret because she hadn't had the guts to put her pride aside and reach out for a man who badly needed love. *Her* love—and their daughter's love. Couldn't she and Rihana help his damaged heart to heal?

'I don't hate you, Hassan,' she said softly. 'In fact, I love you. Even though you didn't want me to love you. And even though you did your best to make me turn my heart against you. I have to tell you that it hasn't worked. And that if you were to ask me to stay here, with Rihana, and to be a proper wife in every sense of the word, then I would do it in a heartbeat. But I will only do it on one condition.'

Her soft and powerful words had momentarily stilled him, but now he stirred because conditions were familiar territory to him. His eyes were wary as they looked at her. 'Which is?'

She swallowed. 'I need to know that you care for *me* in some small way. That there's a small seed of affection in your heart which maybe we can nurture and grow. And that you *will* nurture it, because while I've grown rather fond of the sand which surrounds us, I can't live my life in an emotional desert.'

For long, silent seconds he stared at her, recognising the courage it had taken to lay open her feelings like that. How she humbled him with her courage! His eyes began blinking rapidly and when eventually he could bring himself to speak, his voice sounded strangely hoarse to his ears—the way it had done when he'd had his tonsils removed as a boy. 'Not a seed,' he said brokenly.

'Not a seed?' she repeated in confusion.

He shook his head. 'Not a seed, no, but an eager young plant in its first rapid flush of life. For that is the strength of my "affection" for you, Ella!' A rush of emotion surged through his veins as he reached out and pulled her in his arms. 'But I do not know it by such a mediocre word as *affection*, because for days now I have been realising that it is called something else. Something I have never known before, nor dared to acknowledge.'

'Could you perhaps try acknowledging it now?' she suggested gently, knowing instantly what he meant because she could see it written all over his face. But she needed badly to hear it. She had bared her heart to him and now Hassan needed to redress the balance. To be her equal in every way there was.

He took both her hands in his. 'Ella, I…love you. You hear how my voice falters on these words, but that does not mean you should doubt them. With all my heart and body and mind, I love you. You are everything a woman should be and I do not know why a generous fate should have brought you into my life. You have offered me your heart when I do not deserve—'

'No!' Her fierce word cut him short but her hands were trembling as she reached up to cup his dark and beloved face between her palms. 'You didn't *deserve* the childhood you had and maybe I didn't either. But I think it's time we had some lovely things in our life together, and they are right here at our fingertips. We can reach out and take them any time we want, starting right now. Not palaces or privileges or some flashy lifestyle with *stuff*, but you, me and Rihana.'

'And our marriage will not fail,' he declared softly.

'No, it won't—because we won't let it fail,' she agreed shakily. 'We will learn from all the mistakes our parents made and we will give Rihana the kind of childhood that neither of us knew.'

His lips were passionate as he claimed hers in a kiss far deeper than any kiss he'd ever known. It was about more than passion and maybe about even more than love. It was about understanding and forgiving. About commitment and sharing. About making a happy home for the little girl who lay sleeping in her crib.

Bobby Jackson had christened his daughter Cinderella because he'd wanted her to marry a prince and somehow his rather ambitious dream had come true.

But Ella and Hassan had very different aspirations for their little girl, and that was why Rihana's middle name was Hope.

* * * * *

CLASSIC

Harlequin Presents®

COMING NEXT MONTH from Harlequin Presents®
AVAILABLE JUNE 26, 2012

#3071 HEART OF A DESERT WARRIOR
Lucy Monroe
Sheikh Asad needs to secure his legacy, and Iris is the key. Can she resist so determined a seduction?

#3072 SANTINA'S SCANDALOUS PRINCESS
The Santina Crown
Kate Hewitt
Pampered princess Natalia has swapped couture and cocktails for photocopying! How long will she last working for the devilishly handsome Ben Jackson?

#3073 DEFYING DRAKON
The Lyonedes Legacy
Carole Mortimer
Drakon Lyonedes has power, wealth, sex appeal...and any woman he wants! Until beautiful Gemini Bartholomew enters his life, that is...

#3074 CAPTIVE BUT FORBIDDEN
Lynn Raye Harris
Bodyguard Rajesh Vala must protect Veronica—whatever the cost.... But Veronica has always rebelled against commands and isn't making Raj's job easy!

#3075 HIS MAJESTY'S MISTAKE
A Royal Scandal
Jane Porter
Princess Emmeline is everything this desert king shouldn't want... Posing as her twin sister and Makin's secretary, she's playing with fire!

#3076 THE DARK SIDE OF DESIRE
Julia James
Business legend Leon Marantz exudes a dark power that sends shivers through Flavia Lassiter's body—threatening to shatter the icy shell protecting her heart.

Patricia Thayer welcomes you to Larkville, Texas, in THE COWBOY COMES HOME—book 1 in the exciting new 8-book miniseries, THE LARKVILLE LEGACY, *from Harlequin® Romance.*

REACHING THE BANK, Jess climbed down, smiling as she walked her mount to the water. "Wow, I haven't ridden like that in years."

"You're good."

"I'm Clay Calhoun's daughter. I'm supposed to be a good rider."

"You miss him."

She walked with him through the stiff winter grass to the tree. "It's hard to imagine the Double Bar C going on without him. He loved this land." She glanced around the landscape. "Now my brother runs the operation, but he'll be gone awhile." She released a breath. "I have to say we miss his leadership."

He frowned. "Is there anything I can do?"

"Thank you. You're handling Storm—that's a big enough help. It's just that it would be nice to have my brothers and sister here." She looked at him. "Do you have any siblings?"

He shook his head. "None that I know of."

"What about your father?" she asked.

He shook his head. "Never been in my life. I tried for years to track him down, but I never could catch up with him."

He caught the sadness etched on her face. "Johnny, I'm sorry."

He hated pity, especially from her. "Why? You had nothing to do with it. Jake Jameson didn't want to be found, or meet his son." He shrugged. "You can't miss what you've never had. I'm not much of a homebody, either. I guess that's why I like to keep moving."

Jess looked out over the land. "I guess that's where we're different. I've never really moved away from Larkville."

"Why should you want to leave? You have your business here and your home."

She smiled. "I had to fight Dad to live on my own. But I've got a little Calhoun stubbornness, too."

"You got all the beauty."

Johnny came closer, removed her hat and studied her face. "Your eyes are incredible. And your mouth… I could kiss you for hours."

She sucked in a breath and raised her gaze to his. "Johnny… We weren't going to start this."

"Don't look now, darlin', but it's already started."

HREXP0712